THE PUEBLO AFFAIR

Based on a true story

David Johnson

CHAPTER 1

Date: Monday, November 13, 1967
Location: FBI Washington DC Field Office

It was not a particularly good start to the day.

James Spencer sat waiting in his car hoping for a break in the storm. The light drizzle that had begun on his drive into the office that morning had transformed into a full-blown downpour by the time he found his parking spot off Twelfth Street. The wind had picked up considerably, and heavy raindrops were drumming on his car's windshield and roof. He wasn't looking forward to the walk from his car to the entrance of the Old Post Office Pavilion. It was a Monday morning. The date was November 13, 1967. It was 0706 hours.

The car's engine was still running. The radio was on, and the windshield wipers continued to make temporary arcs of vision, revealing a slightly rusted sign that read 'FBI Parking.'

His left hand rested on the steering wheel with his fingers periodically tapping the stitched leather wrapping, while his right hand remained on the Hurst shifter. He was lost in thought, somewhat mesmerized by the rhythmic beating of the rain. The muffled voice from the car speakers barely registered with him until an overly enthusiastic radio DJ jolted him back to reality with an announcement: "And still on top of the charts for the fourth week in a row, here's LULU and 'To Sir with Love'!"

Spencer muttered "Oh, Jesus!" and turned off the radio.

The rain did not appear to be letting up, so he begrudgingly turned off the car and pulled the key from the ignition. He then reached for his fedora from the passenger seat, put it on his head and pulled it down firmly. He considered using his umbrella but quickly dismissed the idea in the face of the strong winds.

Glancing out the driver's side window, Spencer attempted to calculate how wet he would be by the time he reached the building's entrance. If his guess was correct, he would be very wet. He reached for his briefcase from the floor on the passenger side, opened his car door and stepped out into the cold, pouring rain and wind.

"God damn it!" he swore, his words drowned by the storm.

As it turned out, his calculation had been correct. His hat, trench coat, shoes, and the bottom portion of his trousers were completely soaked by the time he reached the lobby. The clock on the wall showed 0715 hours. Spencer stopped briefly just inside the lobby door to shake the water from his hat and stomp his feet before heading to get a cup of coffee.

"Morning, Jimmy. Can I have a large cup of coffee please," he said to the wiry, older, black man with close-cropped white hair standing behind the counter.

"Sure thing, Mr. Spencer. Black as usual?"

"Yes, please."

Smiling, Jimmy responded, "You got it, boss." And then with a more concerned look commented, "Pretty messy out there, huh?"

"Not a fit day for man or beast." Spencer replied. "Did you beat the rain this morning, Jimmy?"

"I sure did. Didn't get a single drop."

"Good for you! Looks like Lady Luck might be on your side today."

With an undertone of melancholy in his voice, Jimmy replied, "I hope so, James, I surely hope so."

“How’s Macy doing?” Spencer asked in a more hushed, gentler tone. “Have the test results come back yet?”

Jimmy’s wife, Macy, had been diagnosed with breast cancer in the early spring, and, following an operation, had been undergoing months of radiotherapy. She had always been a slight woman, and while the radiation treatments were painless, she found herself completely exhausted and battling continual bouts of lymphedema. Jimmy had mentioned just last week that Macy had finally completed her treatments, and he and Macy were awaiting the results of her final tests.

It had been a very hard year for them both. While Jimmy always managed to appear cheerful with his customers, Spencer knew that he was dying inside over what Macy was going through. To add to their emotional distress, the hospital bills had consumed their meager savings, and the second mortgage they were forced to take out on their house just to stay afloat had left them close to bankruptcy. Jimmy had confided in James that they needed a miracle within months, or they would lose their home – the home where they had raised their children and planned to spend the rest of their lives together. Jimmy was distraught just not knowing what he could do.

“We still haven’t heard back on the test results yet, but we’re praying.” His face conveyed his worry.

“I’m praying too, Jimmy.” Spencer responded softly. “Please tell Macy I said hi and give her my love.”

“I will, James. Thank you.”

Jimmy's contagious smile then returned as he sat the paper cup down on the counter, carefully secured the lid and said, "I filled your coffee all the way to the top this morning. Figured you could use an extra boost to warm you up."

"Thanks, Jimmy, you're a gentleman and a scholar."

“Sorry I didn't have any of those foam cups left.” Jimmy continued. “Should have them in this week. Anyway, it's hot so be careful.”

“Thanks again.” Spencer responded to the warning.

“Oh here,” Jimmy added, “take some napkins to hold it with.”

After paying for the coffee, Spencer wrapped the napkins around the cup and carefully picked it up.

“Have a good day, Jimmy, and keep me posted on Macy.”

“You too James.” Jimmy replied. “Now don't go getting yourself into any trouble.”

They both smiled as Spencer turned to make his way across the lobby to join a growing queue for an elevator.

All eyes were on the moving hand within the aesthetic arch above the elevator doors. The hands registered as the elevators passed each descending floor. Everyone shifted their attention to the one that appeared to be moving the fastest. A buzzer signified that it had finally reached the lobby, and when the door opened, everyone crowded in.

Spencer edged toward the back, and as the doors were closing asked if someone could press the fourth-floor button. The elevator began its ascent filled with a selection of cranky, rain soaked, Monday morning commuters pressed together in cramped silence. Amidst the stuffy atmosphere, Spencer noticed a woman attempting to fix her broken umbrella. The wind had obviously caught it and several of the stretchers had broken loose from the rib. A crowded elevator was not the place to try to repair a broken umbrella; she continued undeterred.

Just then, the Muzak selection emanating from the ceiling speakers switched to Steve Allen's *'This could be the start of something big'*.

Spencer noticed that it didn't seem to improve anyone's attitude.

He passed off the collective dour mood of the passengers in the confined compartment and began singing along to the music in his head.

In one hand, he held the piping hot cup of coffee, while his other gripped the handle of a worn, damp, leather briefcase. It would be worth mentioning that beneath his suit jacket, he carried a Smith & Wesson Model 19 Combat Magnum with a 4-inch barrel. He was, assuredly, the heaviest armed passenger in the elevator that morning.

After successive stops at floors two and three – along with the constant shifting about and bumping as passengers pried their way to the front – the elevator reached the fourth floor and the door opened. Spencer stepped out. The door closed behind him and the music stopped, but he continued singing. "*You're lunching at 21, you're watching your diet.*"

After a hesitation: "Damn, what's the next line?" It wasn't coming to him. He stopped singing.

The rented fourth and fifth floors of the Old Post Office Pavilion became the new headquarters for the FBI Washington Field Office (WFO) in 1951. While the rest of the world was still recovering from World War II and guardedly hoping that the end of Fascism, Nazism, and Japanese imperialism would keep the global threats at bay, North Korea took the opportunity to invade South Korea. It was on June 25th, 1950.

History has taught us that wars are, unfortunately, inevitable, with only the time between them being the variable. In this case, the Korean War began just five years after the end of WWII.

During the ongoing battles, North Korea's leader Kim Il-Sung had the backing of both the U.S.S.R. and China. The FBI, as a result, clearly had their work cut out for them with these three dangerous adversaries more pronounced on their radar.

One of the primary undertakings of the FBI Washington Field Office was counterintelligence. They were responsible for preventing foreign entities from gathering intelligence, spying, assassinations, and carrying out acts of sabotage. It was a challenging and demanding responsibility that was of paramount importance for national security. As the international threats continued to grow, new agents were recruited, and the bureau's resulting requirement for additional office space led to their move to this new location.

James Spencer had been transferred to Washington DC from the New York City office in 1958. His proven and field-tested expertise in counterintelligence, and his outstanding work history were the main, documented, factors behind the approval of his move, but it was felt that rumors floating around the NYC office concerning his possible involvement in the murders of three mafia hitmen who were believed to have killed his wife, probably had some bearing on his transfer. Despite any actual evidence, his superiors decided it was best to expedite the move.

As it turned out, Spencer was a perfect fit for his new position in Washington and the rumors back in NYC quickly became a thing of the past. His track record of solving cases and presenting the U.S Attorney's office with the unequivocal evidence needed to secure convictions continued in Washington and quickly made him one of the top agents in the WFO.

Because of his determination to follow the facts and not let the bad guys slip away on his watch, Spencer earned a reputation for being tenacious – which, in fact, he was. It was a trait that he seemed to have been born with. This determination paid off with a well-deserved promotion to Special Agent.

Spencer walked down the hall that morning focused solely on not spilling the coffee. When he reached his office he set his briefcase on the floor, took his keys from his trench coat pocket and unlocked the door. He glanced behind him at the clock on the wall that was hanging just across the hall from his office door. It was 0729. He took note and then picked up his briefcase and walked into the room. After placing his briefcase on the floor, he carefully set the hot coffee on his desk along with his keys.

Spencer removed his hat, shook it several times and placed it on the shelf of the coat rack standing next to the door. Glancing at the soaked fedora, he realized how far it had strayed from its original, pristine condition. He considered picking up a new one - it was a thought that passed quickly. He removed his still wet trench coat, shook it soundly, and hung it on the rack.

Spencer was fortunate to have his own office – a fact that irked many of the agents who shared the common areas. An office had become available and because of his standing among the Special Agents he was given the first opportunity to claim it.

The office, as it turned out, was somewhat small and cramped; certainly nothing to write home about. The paint on the door and window frames was chipped; several pieces of tile on the floor were cracked or missing; and moisture, age, or both, had caused the walls to take on varying degrees of their original color. A touchup was long overdue, but the condition of the room wasn't of a particular concern to Spencer. He was just relieved to be away from the constant noise on the floor. The wooden desk, a bookcase, the coat rack, and two other chairs, besides his, completed the office decor.

Except for the framed documents hung on the walls.

There were over a dozen varying sized frames displaying letters of commendation and awards. They weren't meant to be displayed to impress anyone, but to him they represented his membership in an organization that he had admired since his days in grade school. He was immensely proud to be a Special Agent with the FBI.

As he turned back to his desk, the sound of traffic on Pennsylvania Avenue caught his attention. He glanced out the window at the growing backup of cars on 12th Street and was glad he had missed the morning rush.

He pulled his leather chair back from the desk and sat down. He then picked up his keys and put them in his jacket pocket. Reaching for his coffee cup he pulled it gently toward him and carefully removed the lid. He then leaned over and sipped from the brim without lifting the cup.

"Morning, Spencer," a passing agent, Mark Williams, called out as he continued walking.

"Good morning," Spencer replied.

Williams continued his way down the hall.

Spencer didn't like Williams – actually, he thought him to be pretty much an ass. It was an assessment he had developed within ten minutes of first meeting the man, and one that was shared by almost every other agent in the WFO. It was common knowledge that he would throw anyone under the bus if it meant putting himself in a better light with management. And it was everyone's assumption that Williams hadn't already been transferred to some obscure branch office in the middle of nowhere because he constantly provided the boss with gossip about the others in the department. Seeing the two of them chatting in the hall never failed to elicit head shakes, eye rolls and mumbled profanities from anyone who happened by.

Just then, the phone rang. "Ah, the day begins," he thought as he answered the call.

The conversation ended and Spencer hung up. He glanced at his current active files and picked up the one he had been working on Friday afternoon before he had left for the weekend. It was labeled Buzzelli. It was time to get to work.

The next several hours were uneventful as he focused on the investigation in the opened file in front of him. Then, as he was taking a final sip of what was now cold coffee, a parade of car horns drew his attention again to the window. It was probably more of an excuse to get away from the desk for a moment then it was to see what the commotion was about, but he stood up and looked out. By the time he glanced down to the street the horns had stopped, and the cars were again moving at a slow, but steady, pace. He took a few deep breaths, stretched his arms and then turned back to his desk.

It was then that he noticed what appeared to be the corner of an envelope protruding from the left pocket of his trench coat. He walked to the coat rack and slowly removed it.

“What the hell is this?” he asked himself.

He sat down, leaned forward in his chair, and with his elbows resting on the desk held the envelope with both hands. It was a sealed, white, folded, business size envelope with no writing on either side. He slowly spun his chair around and held the envelope toward the window attempting to use it as a back light to see what it might contain. The light coming in the window wasn’t particularly bright, but it was enough to see that a letter was enclosed.

"How the hell did this end up in my pocket?" he wondered. His coat pockets were empty when he had left his apartment that morning.

He mentally traced his morning activity. He was alone in his apartment garage. He hadn't passed anyone walking into the building and he was never closer than four or five feet from anyone in the lobby when he arrived. And he was the only one at Jimmy's when he picked up his coffee.

Then he remembered: The elevator.

Someone in the crowded elevator must have slipped it into his pocket. He tried to recall if anyone had seemed out of place on the ride to the fourth floor, but his focus at the time was on the hot coffee.

Having spent years chasing men and women who would think nothing of adding a drop of sarin to your afternoon martini at the Round Robin, he treated the envelope with conditioned caution. Opening his top desk drawer, he removed a pearl handled, inscribed, letter opener – a ten-year service employee gift from the bureau.

He held the envelope at arm's length and inserted the opener between the flap and the envelope body and slowly slit it lengthwise. He was very careful. It was not his intention to be found that morning slumped over his desk with one dead hand clasping a poison laced envelope, and the other wrapped around the pearl handled letter opener presented to him for ten years of vigilant work in counterintelligence.

Holding the opened envelope, still at arm's length, he tipped it slowly over the legal writing pad on his desk to release any possible powered toxins. There were none. Then, out of habit more than anything else, he slowly brought it near his nose to test for any possible slight garlic smell of arsenic or bitter almond of cyanide. There were neither.

Leaning back in his chair, he opened the envelope and removed a single, folded, mimeographed document with a small paper clipped note attached. He removed the note and read it. It was handwritten with the message: 'FYEO. Do not discuss with anyone'. It included a local phone number that he recognized was from the DC area, but not a number he was familiar with.

Spencer laid the small note on his desk and unfolded the document. He was shocked to see that he was holding a copy of a Top-Secret British MI6 intelligence analysis report. He read the document. The report, dated November 3, 1967, detailed a very recent account of an unknown individual providing Top Secret United States cryptographic equipment code key lists to the Soviet Embassy in Washington DC.

The individual was defined as an embassy walk-in who was being handled directly by the Station Chief of the Soviet Embassy, Boris Solomatin. Spencer was very familiar with Solomatin, and the fact that he was overseeing the contact personally was highly unusual. For the Station Chief of the Soviet Embassy to be directly involved, the contact would have to be providing information of the highest strategic importance to the Soviets. United States cryptographic code key lists needed to decipher top secret government communications would certainly warrant his attention.

Spencer held the document in his hands knowing that, if authentic, the information could only have come from an embedded mole in the close inner circle of the Soviet intelligence community.

He was perplexed as to why the document had been given to him. Why hadn't it been delivered to the Director in Charge at the WFO or directly to the Deputy Director or Director of the Bureau? A document of this significance would never go to a Special Agent. And he questioned the 'For Your Eyes Only' notation. None of this made sense to him.

Bureau protocol dictated that he immediately notify his superior of the document; however, his instinct told him to set protocol aside until he knew more. His gut and his judgment were telling him not to pass along any of this information - at least not yet.

After a second review of the analysis report and small note, he got up, walked to his door and quietly closed it. He sat down again, listened to make sure no one was just outside, within earshot, and then picked up the phone and dialed the number on the note. The call was answered on the second ring.

A male voice with a British accent said, “Hello?”

“I have a note with this phone number.” Spencer replied.

“Good, then you found the envelope. It is extremely important that we meet.”

“What’s this all about?” Spencer asked.

“I will bring you up to date personally, not over the phone. But we must meet properly, soon. Do you know the Tune Inn?”

Spencer thought for a moment and then questioned, “The Tune Inn. That’s on Pennsylvania between Third and Fourth, isn't it?”

"Yes, that's it. Meet me there at 1400 hours this afternoon."

His voice was controlled, yet Spencer sensed an urgency and concern.

Spencer asked, "How will I recognize you?"

The man didn't answer directly, but in a slow, deliberate, hushed tone continued,
"This information is to be kept in the strictest confidence. Do not let anyone see the document and do not discuss this information with anyone – particularly anyone at the bureau. This is extremely important. I need your assurance on that."

"This information stays with me. But how will..." Spencer began but was interrupted.

"I'll find you." The line went dead.

Spencer slowly placed the handset back into the phone cradle. He glanced again at the document. If this document were authentic, and it appeared to be, the implications, at numerous levels, were frightening. He slipped the analysis report and the note back into the envelope and placed it in his top desk drawer. He hesitated momentarily, then pulled his keys out of his pocket and locked the drawer. Not that it was common for anyone to be caught looking through the desk of an FBI Special Agent, but the magnitude of the importance of the document seemed to dictate a locked desk.

He glanced up through his door window. In the hallway, a large, brown General Electric wall clock was hanging adjacent to his office door. It was 1123 hours.

He was focused on the clock when a tap on the door window pulled him back to the moment. It was Sheila Anderson. He smiled and waved her in.

Agent Sheila Anderson had begun working at the Washington Field Office a year after Spencer had transferred in. Unlike Spencer, who had set his sights early on becoming an FBI agent, her path to the Bureau was like most others – it wasn't her first choice of occupation. Following high school she attended Brown University, graduating with a double major in international finance and languages, and then quickly found a position with banking giant JP Morgan.

Although she had advanced rapidly in the ranks, she very quickly found the work to be monotonous and boring. She continued working at what she came to refer to as her mundane labor job for only a few years before she began searching for a more exciting career.

It was on the Tuesday of the second week of her job hunting that she happened upon a newspaper article in the Post covering a story that the FBI was looking for educated and talented people.

It immediately caught her attention. With her degree in finance and languages, and her experience at JP Morgan she felt that she might be a good candidate. Her resume was in the mail the following morning.

A postmarked letter from the FBI arrived two weeks later, and following several interviews, she found herself stepping from a chartered bus at the FBI training center in Quantico, Virginia. Her new, exciting career had begun.

She eagerly completed the often grueling twenty-week basic field training course, a course that included an obligatory requirement to be blasted in the face with oleoresin capsicum – pepper spray – and then immediately forced to defend yourself from a trainer who was trying to remove your pistol from its holster. She quite skillfully defended herself while almost totally blind and went on to graduate near the top of her class. Sheila was awarded her FBI badge and credentials and was directed to report to the Washington field office where she began her two-year probation period. Following her probation, she was moved to focus on international money laundering. It was then that she had her first occasion to work with the man whose door she was now standing in front of.

As a result of her position, she and Spencer had had the opportunity to work together regularly. Sheila was brilliant and quickly became his most trusted associate at the bureau. They had become very close personal friends.

When they first began working together, their business affiliation was uniquely melded during their initial investigation as a team. During that investigation it had become apparent that one other agent in the bureau was privy to material in confidential case files that should have been available only to them. That agent was Mark Williams.

Because his meddling could easily impact their work, they discussed several options of how they might address his intrusion. The thought of confronting Williams was off the table. Filing a complaint with his boss – who was most likely already fully aware of his actions – would only bring them unnecessary attention and place them in a forced position to prove their charges: a situation that could prove very awkward and, more importantly, very time-consuming. Time was a crucial element neither one could afford to waste.

Considering their options, they came to the realization that if certain confidential files weren't available for Williams to find, their problem could be resolved without all the grief.

From that point forward James and Sheila secretly agreed to bypass filing documents on certain aspects of their investigations. This, of course, was completely against bureau guidelines, but they stayed the course. It worked brilliantly. The files would appear only after they had completed their investigations and were ready to present the case for prosecution. They continued to close cases and Williams was left without the fodder to impress his boss.

Sheila opened Spencer's door, leaned in and asked, "Do you still need that file on the Buzzelli investigation by this afternoon? I just got a call from Jameson who asked me to attend a finance meeting after lunch. The rumors are that our department is spending too much of the overall budget, so my guess is that it might run a while. I haven't finished pulling the file together yet. Would tomorrow morning be, ok?"

Spencer assured her that the next morning would be fine. His afternoon had taken a different turn and the Buzzelli case was the last thing on his mind.

"That's no problem at all Sheila. And have fun at your meeting," he smiled.

She lowered her head, her face frowning as she looked over the top rim of her glasses. "An afternoon at a table with a couple of bean counters explaining how they could do our job for half the amount we spend. Oh, it will just be delightful, I'm sure."

She shrugged her shoulders and continued, "I am so tired of having to be the one to represent the department at these things."

Spencer smiled and said, "Hey, if you guys stopped flying first class and staying at the 5-star hotels you could avoid all of this. But actually, my guess is they just want someone pretty to class up the room."

"Well, James, if I could get ahead on just my amazing looks," she said, now smiling as she tossed her hair back, "I would be sitting in J. Edward's chair right now running this place."

Spencer laughed and said: "Sheila, didn't your mother ever tell you never try to look prettier than the bride at the wedding?"

"O, my god. I hope no one overheard this conversation," she said laughing!

"We're safe. Now quit your whining and go to the meeting. I'm sure you will do your department proud."

Smiling, she said "See ya," pulled the door closed and then turned and walked down the hall.

Spencer glanced at the clock again. Get back to work, he thought.

The next two hours passed with no additional interruptions, but he could focus on nothing except the document. When it was time to head to the Tune Inn, he unlocked the desk drawer, pulled the envelope out and put it in his inside suit jacket pocket. He then reached under his suit jacket and briefly, reassuringly, gripped the handle of his revolver.

To prevent encountering anyone inside the building, he opted to forgo the elevator and proceeded to a designated 'exit' door, making his way down the stairs. The door at the bottom landing on the ground floor opened around the corner from the front entrance of the building – a more unnoticed egress. As he stepped out, he found that the rain and wind had subsided only a little from that morning. He pulled his coat tight at the neck, pulled his hat brim low on his face and walked around the corner to Pennsylvania. A cab was just letting off a couple. He walked directly to the cab and got in. "Pennsylvania and Forth, please," Spencer told the driver.

He purposely directed to be dropped off a block past the restaurant. It was mid-afternoon and the traffic was heavy and moving slowly. Spencer spent the time anticipating what to expect. The cab stopped.

"Here you go, buddy," the driver barked.

Spencer paid the fare and got out.

He stopped at the light on Fourth and quickly observed his surroundings. The few pedestrians who had braved the still ongoing wind and rain seemed focused on getting to where they were headed and out of the elements. As the light changed, he crossed the street and headed directly to the Tune Inn and walked in the front door.

The smell of burgers, French fries and beer greeted him.

Tune Inn was a long, narrow restaurant with a bar just inside the door on the left. An elderly man sat somewhat unsteadily on the bar stool nearest the front door. A cane was leaned against the bar next to him. He was holding a glass of whiskey with a trembling hand. His hair was white and thin and windblown. His gaze was down.

Tables and booths ran along both walls just as you passed the bar, and the entire length of the room was adorned with the mounted heads of animals that had been hunted by the owners of the inn. The remaining wall space was decorated with old photographs, and memorabilia. A television sat precariously on a shelf above the bar. It was turned on but ignored by everyone.

The Tune Inn was a popular spot for locals and the occasional congressman who wanted to remember how the little people lived. Spencer hadn't been there for several years. He noticed that the only thing that seemed to have changed was the faces of the patrons. This afternoon, following the lunch rush, he found the bar to be nearly empty; a fact that his contact obviously had taken into consideration.

Three women sat at the only occupied table. Their coats were draped over the back of the empty chair that had been pulled back, and several shopping bags from upscale shops were sitting on the empty seat. One of the ladies was older and Spencer surmised by their conversation that the other two were her daughters and they were treating her to a day of shopping and lunch.

And only two of the booths were taken. The first, which was near the bar, was occupied with what looked to be a family of tourists, discussing which museum they would visit next. In the booth at the rear of the restaurant sat a man with his back to the front door.

Spencer walked toward the back booth. As he got closer, the man lifted his left hand to signal him. He had obviously seen him enter by his reflection in the glass of a large picture hanging on the wall.

Before he sat down, Spencer quickly glanced again around the room looking for available exits – a habit that had helped save him in numerous compromising situations over the years. He noticed that the elderly man at the bar was still lost in what must have been sad, lonely thoughts; the three ladies were still occupied in quiet discussion; and the spirited family still couldn't decide between the Washington monument or the Museum of Natural History. A decision Spencer guessed would be determined by the weather.

The room appeared secure. He sat down.

The man in the booth lifted his drink, looked at Spencer and nodded slightly. A drink had already been placed in front of Spencer.

"I assume you still drink Scotch?" the man asked.

The question immediately raised Spencer's sense of vulnerability.

Spencer studied his companion, thinking he must know him, but did not.

"Yes, Scotch is fine. We have obviously met?" It was more of a statement than a question.

Their conversation was hushed.

"Yes, we have James, but just briefly several years ago. My name is Sidwell, Allston Sidwell. It was in London. SIS had requested assistance on tracking an American, a rather nasty chap, who was working with the KGB and saw no problem picking off our agents with a rifle from rooftops in various cities around the world. You were working with one of my people on the case, Philip Hanson."

Sidwell sat his glass on the table and continued.

"I chanced upon you both having drinks following the capture of the swine. We had our cordial introductions and Philip asked if I could join you for a scotch. Unfortunately, I had pending business, so we parted ways"

Spencer interjected: "I do remember that case and our brief introduction."

Sidwell continued. "It is a habit of mine to follow-up meticulously on the filed paperwork of my people. In doing so on that case, it came to my attention that your work was exceptional. In fact, we might still be looking for the rifleman if it weren't for you. I don't believe I had ever seen such attention to detail and logical skill before."

The disconnect between the MI6 memo that brought him to the Tune Inn and a brief encounter from several years past on a completely unrelated case only added to the confusion.

"What is this all about? How did you find me and what does the report you put in my pocket have to do with me?" Spencer asked.

Sidwell leaned forward and lowered his voice further. "I'm with British MI5. Finding people is one of the things we do very well." There was something about Sidwell's tone that had a foreboding undercurrent pulling things back to the dark reality of their work.

"You have obviously read the document," Sidwell said.

"Yes, of course," Spencer replied.

"There is more to the story. Unfortunately, our contact who provided the information in the document, is missing. But our last communications with him led us to believe that the walk-in who is providing the crypto key lists is an enlisted sailor stationed at the Norfolk Naval Station in Virginia. The code key lists are for a top-secret encryption device labeled KL-47. If the Soviets have the code lists, they can configure the KL-47 to decipher top secret Naval communications. We had nothing other than our agents reports, but it was more than enough for our top command to notify your Naval command and the FBI."

"If they have this information, why are you involving me?" Spencer asked.

"That's what makes this a sticky wicket James. The information is going nowhere. Our reply from your country was directly from the Office of the Secretary of the Navy. They stated that they had done a thorough investigation concerning the possible theft of secret Crypto key lists, and they had determined that there was no reason to believe the MI6 informants' information was correct. They, of course, added that any further investigation could lead to an international incident with the Soviets, and they wanted to avoid that at any cost."

"What about the FBI?" Spencer questioned.

"They responded that following an investigation they had found no reason to question the Navy's findings."

"Is it possible the MI6 report was wrong?" Spencer followed up.

"Our contact has never been wrong before. I firmly believe that cryptographic coding key lists are being delivered to the Soviet Embassy, and your Navy and FBI have decided to deep six this."

Spencer sat quietly, focused.

"Your Navy transmits coded operational intelligence broadcast messages of all naval war ship deployment and missions along with top secret updates on military actions and directives across the world. If the KL-47 code key lists got into the hands of the Soviets, they would be hand delivered your entire game plan for naval military action across the world. This would have frightening consequences for not only the United States, but Britain, and the rest of the free world. This scoundrel must be found and eliminated."

"Wouldn't they need the KL-47 crypto machine to utilize the key lists?" Spencer inquired.

"They would, but we cannot be sure that they don't already have the machine in their possession. We know that several of your systems have been decommissioned because the hardware has fallen into enemy hands, but some of those did not come to light until months later. And, it is not to say copies of engineering documents might have been made available and the Soviets have constructed their own."

"Jesus," Spencer replied. They both took another sip of scotch.

"Why the hell would the Navy and FBI cover this up?" Spencer asked somewhat incredulously.

Sidwell lowered his voice a bit more.

"We know that the directive to close this down is coming from the White House. Lyndon Johnson has been briefed on our intelligence reports concerning this Norfolk spy, and he, unfortunately, is focused only on the political implications surrounding it that could affect him directly. His polling numbers are in the toilet, and he is fighting for his political life. His chances of winning the nomination for the next election are almost nonexistent, but he isn't sold on that yet and will do anything to avoid any additional negative reporting. Viet Nam has tarnished his legacy severely and he doesn't need news of a spy in the Navy tarnishing it even more. We know that he is adamant to make sure this just disappears. He has put immense pressure on both of our governments to step away from this."

Spencer remained intently listening, showing no emotion.

"James, perhaps I could put this a bit more diplomatically, but the fact is Lyndon Johnson is an arrogant, son-of-a-bitch who quite frankly doesn't care what it takes to keep this all quiet."

"Hoover, I'm assuming, is also aware of your intelligence reports," Spencer added.

"According to our information, it has reached his desk, so, yes, he is. Hoover has managed to hold his position in the Bureau through eight presidents because he caters completely to whoever happens to be in the White House. Johnson has most certainly spoken to him, so you will be stopped immediately if you mention this to any one higher up the chain in the Bureau."

Sidwell picked up his glass again and slowly took a sip of scotch.

He then looked directly at Spencer.

"They will stop at nothing to make this go away James; absolutely nothing."

Spencer grasped the meaning.

"Why are you telling me all of this?" Spencer asked. "What do you expect me to do?"

"You are a top-rated agent in the WFO, you are a stickler for following facts wherever they lead, you have a strong belief in upholding the laws of your country. And, if I am not mistaken, you have stepped outside the constraints of the FBI before to take things into your own hands if necessary."

There was a brief silence as Spencer studied Sidwell's face, looking for some hint of an explanation to his last comment.

"Forgetting the political pressure to hide this, James, it is a matter of global security, and we need someone willing to do whatever is necessary to stop the Navy spy. We need to get around your top brass. That's why I am reaching out to you. You may be our only option."

They both lifted their glasses and took another sip of scotch.

"What makes you think I won't go back and report our meeting here this afternoon?" Spencer asked.

"Will you?" Sidwell inquired.

Spencer sat quietly for a moment and then replied, "No."

"Then I have picked the right man haven't I James."

Sidwell slowly set the glass on the table and continued.

"I am most certainly being followed, James. According to SIS, they no longer have any record of this entire incident, and MI6, officially, is dropping this investigation. But I would be naive to think that there aren't people in SIS who suspect me in these efforts and are trying to stop me. My flight here was under an assumed name, of course, and it will take them some time to catch up. But they will. I would hope that I can make my flight out this evening before my whereabouts is discovered. My flight is scheduled at 8:45."

"Won't you be stopped immediately when you arrive back in England?"

"I won't be returning to England."

Spencer did not continue. He understood.

"Can I count on you to consider what is at play here and follow through, James?"

Spencer wasn't sure why he nodded his head in agreement, but he did.

"Good," Sidwell replied. "The ball is now in your court. Guard it."

Sidwell picked up his glass and slowly finished the remaining scotch. He sat the empty glass on the table and reached out his hand. As they shook hands he continued. "Thank you, James. Good luck and Godspeed."

As Spencer watched him stand and walk out of the bar, his mind was a kaleidoscope of confused and disturbing images and thoughts. He picked up his glass and drank the remainder of the whisky. When he felt that it was an appropriate amount of time, he stood up and walked out of the Tune Inn.

Turning to his left, he walked down the street a block before flagging a cab. He pulled the cab door closed and told the driver "Old Post Office Pavilion."

The driver responded with "No problem."

As the cab pulled away from the curb, Spencer collapsed back in the seat. He closed his eyes and then from out of nowhere, began singing quietly:

"Declining a charlotte russe, accepting a fig."

"What's that?" the cabbie questioned.

"Oh, nothing, just a song I heard this morning." Spencer replied.

The remainder of the trip was in silence.

CHAPTER 2

Tuesday morning, November 14, 1967

The pulsating squeal of a police car siren woke Spencer from the restless night he had endured in his living room recliner. His eyes remained closed as his muddled thoughts attempted to develop some form of structure. He slowly opened his eyes and squinted to the left at the bottle of Dewar's sitting on the table. He realized then that he should have stopped drinking much earlier than he had.

"What was I thinking? Jesus!"

Through the pounding in his head, he could vaguely remember spending the past evening going over every possible scenario that might have made sense to the previous day – there had been no good scenarios. He had even tried to convince himself that the answers would unfold when he arrived at work that morning, and all would be well again, but in all honesty, he knew that probably wasn't going to be the case.

As the siren faded into the distance, he glanced at his watch. Once focused, he realized that he was running late.

Passing briefly over the thought that the hair of the dog might be a valid hangover cure in this situation, he skipped a pour of scotch and grudgingly pulled himself out of the chair. His expectations for the day were very low.

Spencer's efforts at showering and dressing could be defined as little more than going through the motions. He haphazardly ransacked through his medicine cabinet looking for a bottle of aspirin, but with no luck. He felt like hell. He didn't look much better.

He strapped his shoulder holster in place, put on his coat and hat, grabbed his briefcase, picked up his keys and headed to the apartment parking garage. It was a quiet ride in to work. The radio was off. He did very little thinking.

Spencer arrived at his desk that Tuesday morning with his usual cup of coffee, along with a Boston cream doughnut that had somehow seemed appealing when he saw it at the coffee stand. This morning, he was glad Jimmy had again filled the cup to the brim. He was going to need it. And he was thankful the Styrofoam cups were available.

He opened his top desk drawer and removed a tin of Bayer aspirin that had been rattling around in it since he had moved into his office years before. After fumbling a bit, he finally squeezed the tin on the correct corner to open it and dumped the remaining four tablets in his hand. He swallowed the pain killer, which was years past its expiration date and likely useless, with several sips of coffee. He then picked up the doughnut and took a bite. The phone rang.

"Oh shit!" he mumbled while trying to quickly swallow. Taking another swig of coffee to wash it down he answered the phone on the third ring.

"This is Spencer."

His immediate boss, Supervisory Special Agent, Tom Carson announced (his phone conversations were never conversations – just announcements), "For a minute I didn't think you were in. Glad I was wrong. Look James, I need you to follow up on something quickly. Stop in my office for a second."

Spencer responded, "Be right there." He slowly maneuvered out of his chair and headed to Carson's corner office, hoping, again, that the word of the spy out of Norfolk had reached Carson's desk and he was going to bring him up to speed on it.

That, he was to find out, wasn't the case.

Spencer knocked on the closed door and opened it slightly. Carson was on the phone. He looked up briefly and waived Spencer in. Carson's lit cigarette was smoldering in the ashtray while he played with his Zippo lighter, spinning it on his desk. He did that a lot. It was a trait of Carson's that Spencer found annoying. Carson stopped playing with the lighter and reached for his pack of Chesterfields offering one to Spencer. Spencer declined with a head shake.

Carson hurried the call and hung up. He picked up his cigarette, as if he was going to take a drag, but instead flicked off the ash several times, put it back in the ashtray and looked up.

"Jesus, you look like hell James. You don't have the flu, do you?"

Before Spencer could respond Carson continued.

"We've got a problem. There was a shooting at the Hay-Adams hotel last night and metro called to give us a heads up. They said the guy they found was well dressed and his over coat and suit jacket had a London manufacture label, but they couldn't find a wallet or passport, and there was no suitcase. And the name he used to check in at registration couldn't be traced. And to add to that, their guys found an unspent cartridge under the bed. It was a foreign manufacture, and a quick check makes them think it was for a Webley 38."

Spencer kept his bloodshot eyes fixed on Carson, saying nothing.

"A British-manufactured cartridge at the scene of a murder,

along with the other questions, could put this in our ballpark James. Head over there now and let's get this sorted out. Maybe it's nothing, but I notified the guys upstairs to give them an update just in case. They're going to be calling back, and as soon as I hear from them, I'll give you a call at the hotel to let you know how they want us to handle it."

While Carson was jotting down some notes on a small piece of paper, he said, "God knows what you're going to find, but if there is some international connection, whatever, we damn well better get on top of it quick. I don't need the brass coming down on me if we were to miss something like that. Those bastards would be looking for a scapegoat and it sure as hell isn't going to be me. Let's get this cleaned up quick."

Carson leaned forward and reached his hand out over his desk to pass the note to Spencer.

"The Metro guys already know you're headed over."

Spencer stepped forward and took the paper. His mind was reeling, as he cautiously asked: "Do you have the name from registration?"

"It's in the note there," Carson said pointing to the paper in Spencer's hand. "Blakeman, I think. Yeah, that was it, Blakeman, Howard Blakeman. Hay-Adams across from Lafayette Square, you know where it is."

Spencer lowered his gaze to the paper he was holding.

"Oh, keep this as low key as possible. A murder at the Hay-Adams is not particularly good for their business."

Carson's phone rang and he reached to pick it up.

"Carson. Oh, hello Jim, thanks for calling back. Hang on one second, would you?"

Spencer was still standing in front of the desk looking at the note. Carson looked up at Spencer and asked anxiously: "You have a question, James?"

"No. No. Looks like I've got what I need here."

There were plenty of questions racing through Spencer's mind, but he turned and walked out of the office. It was obvious that Carson was unaware of the top-secret MI6 document that outlined the spy in Norfolk.

Spencer walked numbly back to his office and collapsed in his chair. The guttural force of the words 'Jesus Christ!' coincided with his almost defeated landing.

If this did turn out to be Sidwell's body in the hotel, Sidwell had been correct. He was being followed. Spencer's own implication in this mess became acutely obvious.

Sidwell's warning that 'they would stop at nothing to make sure it stays hidden' raised the hair on the back of his neck. Could someone know of their meeting at the 'Tune Inn' the day before? Spencer decided his best move would be to assume no one knew of his relationship with Sidwell. He would head to the hotel and wait for Carson's phone call.

He took another bite of the donut, followed by a couple of swigs of coffee. He would have loved to have just finished both, but they would have to wait.

He stood up, glanced out the window and repeated what still seemed to be the appropriate sentiment for the moment? "Jesus Christ!"

Spencer took his trench coat and hat from the rack and put them on. He then reached under his jacket, grabbed the handle of his Smith & Wesson and removed the weapon, opening the cylinder to reconfirm it was loaded. Satisfied, he slipped it back into the worn, steer hide holster, buttoned his coat and headed to the hotel.

The Hay-Adams was about six blocks away. Instead of driving himself, he flagged down a cab. Parking at the hotel wasn't something he wanted to fight with that morning. He stepped from the cab and walked into the front door of the Hay-Adams.

"Agent Spencer," a man Spencer recognized as a metro police lieutenant, called out. Spencer walked toward the lieutenant and reached out his hand.

As they shook hands, the lieutenant said, "Not sure if you remember me, but we worked together on that double homicide near the Capitol last year."

"I do," Spencer replied. "Johnson, isn't it?"

"Yes, Tim Johnson. The station called to say you would be coming. Thanks for getting here so fast. Let me take you up to the crime scene."

Spencer followed him to the elevator, and they rode to the third floor.

When the elevator door closed, and it was only the two of them, Johnson said, "The shooting was in room 342. It looks like it might have been a tourist who got tied up in a robbery that went bad. There was no sign of a break-in so I'm guessing the suspect met the guy either in the elevator or the hallway and followed him to his room. Poor guy just happened to be in the wrong place at the wrong time. Doesn't look like much more than that to me, but when we found the cartridge, I just thought it might be a good idea to give you guys a call. Hey if this looks like something that might fall under Federal jurisdiction, I would be more than happy to turn it over to you. We've got three guys out with the flu, and we had two other homicides and a shooting in the city last night, so our resources are kind of stretched."

Spencer looked at the lieutenant, realizing that he had no concept of what might have transpired. He said nothing in response but shook his head a couple of times to acknowledge Johnson's comments.

“The medical examiner arrived about 15 minutes ago, so he might be able to add something,” Johnson noted.

They got to the room and walked in. Blood, bone, and brain matter were splattered across the headboard and white duvet covering the bed.

It’s not that Spencer wasn’t accustomed to seeing disturbing crime scenes, but this one was different. The victim was lying on his back on the floor near the end of the bed. The blood pattern suggested that he had fallen forward onto the bed after he was shot and then was pulled off the bed and flipped over to be searched. He was still wearing his trench coat that was sprawled open across the floor on either side of him. All the pockets had been pulled inside out. The medical examiner was kneeling next to the body, hiding the victim’s face.

Spencer stepped forward, hoping; but knowing better.

It was Sidwell.

A gaping wound in his forehead defined the bullet exit. It was obviously a large caliber. Death was instantaneous. Spencer had been prepared to find that his contact from the Tune Inn, the day before, was the man who had been killed, but he was shaken none the less. He stood staring.

“Sorry, can I get in here to get a few more pictures?” a man with an official looking camera asked.

“Sorry,” Spencer said as he stepped back out of the way.

The all business like, somewhat aloof, kneeling medical examiner, who was now holding up Sidwell’s head and looking under it said, "Lieutenant, this guy seems to have been shot from behind at close range, but there are very few signs of muzzle flash on his hair or clothes. It doesn't make sense, unless the killer was using a suppressor. And how many local thugs are using suppressors?"

Johnson ignored the analysis of the examiner but replied, "thanks Doctor."

Spencer didn't ignore the Doctor's analysis though – he had expected as much.

"I'm guessing he died somewhere between 4 and 5 last night. I'll have a better feel once we get him back for the autopsy." The doctor returned to the body.

Spencer turned to Johnson and asked, "And you say there was no suitcase?"

"No."

"No documents of any kind?"

"None."

"OK, thanks," Spencer replied.

"Oh, here's the casing we found," Johnson added as he handed Spencer an evidence envelope with the enclosed bullet casing. He looked at it briefly, and then handed it back to Johnson.

"Have you been able to contact the guests in the rooms on either side and across the hall to see if anybody heard or saw anything?" Spencer inquired.

Neither of the rooms on either side was occupied. Apparently, there was a plumbing problem in the room across the hall, and it has been closed for repair since Friday. Nobody in this hall remembers hearing or seeing anything."

Spencer looked around the room, glancing briefly out the tall, curtain framed window with an unobstructed view of the White House across Lafayette Square. The majestic, historic white building seemed oddly surreal as he viewed it from the hotel room, with the bloody, violated body lying at his feet.

The phone in the room rang and Johnson picked it up. "Agent Spencer? Yes, he's here." He handed the phone to Spencer. "It's for you."

Spencer took the handset knowing that his boss was going to tell him that the FBI would be overseeing the investigation. "This is Spencer." He turned slightly away from Johnson as he listened to Carson for several seconds.

"Wait, tell me that again," he said.

He listened as Carson announced that it wasn't a federal case, and they wouldn't be getting involved. It was to be left with the Metro police – obviously nothing more than a mugging and robbery. And he also said; "Just to be safe, bring the cartridge they found back to the office. Tell them we'll run a check on it at the lab, and if anything at all comes up, we'll let them know. I'm sure they'll appreciate the help."

Spencer's knuckles turned white as he squeezed the handset. He knew what had happened here, but was forced to control his urge to say, "What the hell do you mean walk away from this!?"

Spencer knew he couldn't say anything. His involvement with the man lying dead on the floor could never be known.

Instead, he started to ask, "Do you want me to..."

Carson's voice abruptly interrupted Spencer mid-sentence. " "Just turn it over to Metro and get the hell out of there. We don't touch it! And come to my office as soon as you get back." The dial tone indicated that the conversation had ended.

Yesterday, Allston Sidwell, a British MI5 agent had given Spencer a top-secret SIS document defining a spy stationed at Norfolk, VA. They had met at the Tune Inn to discuss the international implications of the information defined in the document. He had told Spencer that both of their governments would stop at nothing to make sure the information on the spy was squelched. Allston Sidwell was now lying dead in a pool of his own blood in a room at the Hay-Adams hotel, and Spencer had just been told that it was of no interest to the FBI. He was absolutely astounded by Carson's instruction. He was shaken to the core. This couldn't all be happening.

Spencer slowly put the handset back in the cradle, unable to release it, as if he was expecting Carson to call back to tell him it was a mistake, and the FBI would, in fact, be taking the lead on the case. The phone didn't ring. He released his clasp and slowly turned toward Johnson.

"Well, looks like you're stuck with this guy after all. Not something we want to get involved with. Guess you were right, some unlucky guy in the wrong place at the wrong time. This one's all yours, lieutenant. Sorry."

The Lieutenant just shrugged his shoulders.

"Hey, if it would help, I can take the casing back and let the hot shots in the lab take a look at it. It's probably nothing, but maybe we can save you guys some time. I can get back to you with the results as soon as they're in."

"Sure, no problem." Johnson replied as he was handing the evidence envelope with the bullet to Spencer. "Appreciate the help. We'll take care of this end. Thanks again for coming over."

Spencer slipped the envelope into his suit jacket pocket.

The Doctor closed his bag and stood up. He glanced down at the body on the floor and said nothing. His expression and head shakes defined his feelings. Another wasted life.

"Doc, if you've got everything you need here, I'll call for a pickup to get this guy moved to the morgue."

"I've got everything I need."

Johnson picked up the phone and began dialing.

After a short conversation he hung up and said to the group, "I'm headed back to the precinct. The bus is on the way."

He then turned to a rather portly police officer and said, "Sergeant Carter, when the bus gets here, make sure they take the body out the service elevator. Don't need to disturb the other guests."

"Understand Sir."

"And keep a couple of your men here until the cleaners get over to sanitize the place. When they're done you can close up the room and let the manager know we're out."

"Will do, Sir."

The Medical Examiner followed Johnson out the door. The few remaining police quietly continued their investigation. The photographer quietly continued to take pictures of the scene.

Spencer made one more visual pass of the room. It was obvious that Metro would wrap this up and pretty much close the files before the week was out. There would be no official investigation requested by British Intelligence because there would be no record that Sidwell had even existed. The only link that Spencer had to the naval spy was most likely headed to an unmarked grave.

He walked out of hotel room 342.

When he stepped out of the front door of the hotel, he noticed that Johnson was just getting into his car.

"Lieutenant, any chance I can catch a ride?"

"Sure, jump in."

The traffic was backed up because of road construction, but the extra time getting back to the office gave Spencer more time to think. "What the hell just happened?" he asked himself. Who could have made the decision to walk away from this?

Johnson dropped him off in front of the building and Spencer took the elevator to the fourth floor. He was glad that he was the only passenger. Small talk wouldn't have gone well. He stepped into his office, removed his hat and overcoat and hung them on the coat rack and headed to Carson's office. The door was closed. He knocked.

After several seconds Carson responded, "Come in."

Spencer opened the door and entered, surprised to see not only Carson but two other men in the room. One was standing next to Carson's desk, and the other was sitting in the chair to the left in front of it. There were no introductions.

"Please take a seat," Carson said. Spencer could see that he was tense and nervous. Spencer sat in the empty chair on the right.

The man standing in a posture of authority next to Carson spoke first. "Agent Spencer, isn't it?"

"Yes," James replied.

"Your boss tells us you've been one of his top agents for quite a few years."

Spencer began to reply, but the man continued talking, ignoring his attempted response.

"We understand that you are known to never let questions go unanswered in a case. That's what makes a good agent now doesn't it?"

Spencer realized that he was not expected to respond during this 'conversation', so he didn't.

"Your records show that you have been a dedicated member of the bureau team, and your excellent work has resulted in numerous commendations and awards."

The man sitting next to Spencer then spoke.

"You have been with the bureau for, what, almost 22 years." It was a statement, not a question. It was obvious they had been through his personnel files.

"I'm guessing you have plans to be with the bureau until you reach full retirement age and then relax with a well-deserved pension. And that's the way it should be."

"Well, look, we just wanted to stop in to meet with you and your boss to make sure we were all on the same page on this guy who was killed last evening. We understand it has absolutely nothing to do with the bureau, so we move on and get back to work."

Spencer sat quietly, his eyes not leaving the man who was talking.

"Agent Spencer, I'm sure you are looking at even more commendations in the coming years before you retire, and we want to make sure we all make it to retirement as a team."

The man standing next to Carson now spoke again. "Agent Spencer, do you have any questions?"

Finally, a chance to speak and all James could say was "No."

The man placed his hand on Carson's shoulder for just a moment and then stepped around the desk toward Spencer and reached out his hand. Spencer stood and they shook hands. As they did, he thanked Spencer for his understanding on this 'situation' and then winked, as a not too subliminal indication that they would be watching him. He then leaned in closer to Spencer and almost whispered, "We all want to make sure we do the right thing here Agent Spencer."

The man then stepped back and said, "I believe you brought something back from the crime scene for the lab to look at. May I have it please?"

Spencer pulled the envelope with the bullet from his coat pocket and handed it to him.

"Thank you, agent. Oh, and we've talked to your boss about an opportunity for you that you just might want to consider. It's time a man of your talents is rewarded for his efforts. And, Agent Spencer, we want you to know that we certainly appreciate everything you do."

The second man then stood, and they walked out of Carson's office.

Carson avoided looking directly at Spencer. As he began shuffling some papers on his desk he said, "Give me a couple of minutes James and I'll stop over to bring you up to date."

Spencer closed the door quietly as he left. He walked back to his office with the knowledge that the rumors of a rogue state operating in the bowels of the FBI had just become so much more than just rumors. There is no way this 'opportunity' was going to be good news.

He sat in his chair staring at the brown clock on the wall in the hall across from his office. He watched the second hand hesitate briefly after each move. It seemed to be moving much slower today.

Spencer had to assume that his clandestine meeting yesterday at the Tune Inn had gone undetected. He is sure that if they had known he met with Sidwell, he would already be in a cooler next to him in the morgue.

Though they had nothing solid, either an unanswered question brought him to their attention or his specific knowledge of the British clothing labels, and the Webley .38 cartridge was enough to place him in their sights.

This came from way higher up the ladder. Carson was right, they would be looking for a scapegoat, and it appeared that he just might fit the bill. They were covering all angles to keep this quiet.

Spencer now knew for sure everything that Sidwell had told him was correct.

The government closed its eyes to a Norfolk Naval Station sailor selling top-secret cryptographic security key lists to the Soviets, and the federal government, the Navy, and the FBI were doing everything to make sure it stayed that way.

None of this made any sense to an experienced, dedicated, career agent of the bureau.

The second hand on the large, brown General Electric clock kept moving and hesitating, moving and hesitating. Spencer's thought turned to the bottle of scotch on the end table next to his recliner in his apartment.

The knock on the door pulled him away from his confused state.

Carson walked in, closed the door behind him, then pulled out a chair in front of Spencer's desk and sat down.

Looking pensively at Spencer, he lifted both hands out in front of him to indicate he wanted control at this point.

"James, for once, I want you to just listen until I'm done. Everything you are about to hear came from upstairs."

"I don't have any idea what happened, or why you're in their sights, but somebody high up wants you as far away from this murder case as possible. I'm not even going to wager a guess why, because whatever it is, I don't want to be involved. I have been directed to present you with two options for your future.

Spencer sat quietly in his chair. His eyes fixed on Carson.

"The Special Agent in Charge in the Honolulu bureau died in a boating accident two weeks ago. There is an open slot for his position. The two men you met in my office suggested that you could be the man to fill that position. It would be a perfect spot to settle into to finish your career in the Bureau. It would be a substantial promotion along with a big jump in pay. The opportunity to finish your career in paradise. It would be perfect, James. And they assured me that the job is yours if you want it."

Spencer sat quietly for a minute, and then asked: "And the second?"

"Second what?" Carson responded with a somewhat startled tone.

"The second option for my future."

Carson's face took on an almost pallor appearance. He stumbled for words. It was obvious he had assumed Spencer would jump at the opportunity in Hawaii.

He then almost blurted out, "The other option is that you turn in you badge now, clean out your office and leave. We can call it an early retirement. Of course, I'll do what I can to make sure you get your benefits and a pension."

Spencer sat quietly.

"Hawaii would be perfect, James. If it were me, I'd take it in a heartbeat."

The room remained silent.

Carson then continued. "You will clean out your desk either way. This is your last day at the WFO. If you take Hawaii, and I hope to God you do, you will have the rest of the week to get things wrapped up at home. We'll have movers in on Friday to pack everything up and get it shipped. Your tickets will be delivered, and you will be on the plane Saturday morning. Your first day at work in Honolulu will be Monday. You can get situated in your new office and catch up on your staff, and then take a week or two off to find an apartment and get settled in. I think you've got plenty of vacation time built up."

Spencer sat quietly.

Carson continued again. This time with a raised voice, "James, I have one year before my pension can kick in. I'm not about to let anything come between me and a secure retirement. You will decide before I leave your office, or I will decide for you. Look, this is all bullshit. We both know that. But in situations like this we all just do what is required to survive."

The room remained quiet.

"I need an answer, James."

Spencer looked up at the clock and then back to Carson. "I'll be on the flight to Hawaii."

"Thank you, James. Thank you."

Carson reached over the desk to shake Spencer's hand. Spencer made no effort to reciprocate.

The extended hand was withdrawn.

"If you stop by my office after you get your personal stuff packed up, I'll bring you up to date as much as I can on the Honolulu position. Do you need some boxes to get everything out?"

"No, I can manage."

Carson turned and left the office, closing the door behind him.

The room became very quiet. It was then that Allston Sidwell's warning came hauntingly back again. "They will stop at nothing to make sure this goes away; absolutely nothing."

Spencer sat in his chair and for the final time looked around his office...the chipped paint around the doors and windows, the faded walls, the inbox still full, and files scattered across his desk. This was all somebody else's problem now.

He pounded both clenched fists on the desk. "Jesus Christ!"

He then slowly got up and began removing the framed letters of commendation and awards from the walls. He removed the first three, carried them to the waste basket next to his desk and gently placed them in it. He continued until his office walls were empty. The trash can was not large enough for all the wall hangings, so he stacked the remainder on the floor next to it.

He then pulled open the top drawer of his desk and removed the pearl handled, inscribed, letter opener – the ten-year service employee gift from the bureau. He slipped it between the framed documents in the waste basket.

Glancing briefly at the empty tin of Bayer aspirin, he slowly closed the drawer.

Spencer walked out of his office for the last time. He carried only his briefcase. He stopped briefly at Carson's office and glanced in the window. Carson was on the phone. There was a cigarette smoldering in the ashtray; he was spinning his Zippo lighter on the desk.

Spencer continued walking.

It was a quiet drive back to his apartment.

CHAPTER 3

Norfolk Naval Station, Virginia
October 1967

One month previous

The distance from Naval Station Norfolk in Hampton Virginia to 1125 16th Street in Washington DC is 192 miles. It was soon to become a well-traveled corridor.

The beautiful Beaux-Arts mansion that occupies the 16th street property was originally known as the Mrs. George Pullman House. Mrs. Pullman (Hattie) had purchased the property in 1909 and then engaged the prominent architect Nathan Wyeth to design the magnificent 64 room edifice that stands there today. Unfortunately, Hattie never had the opportunity to live in the house, although she did make numerous trips to Europe to select only the finest furnishings that would be appropriate for a home of this distinction. The house cost $350,000 to construct, a huge amount in 1909.

But Hattie had the money. She was the widow of Mr. George Pullman. George, one of the great industrialists of the time had made millions of dollars by designing and manufacturing the highly successful Pullman sleeping car for trains. And as a shrewd, powerful businessman who focused solely on profits, he found that he could greatly improve his bottom line by forcing his employees to work for a fraction of what the going pay rate was at the time. George died in 1897 leaving his, somewhat ill-gotten, fortune to his wife.

In 1913, following numerous trips to Europe and the complete furnishing of the home – from the beautiful entry way with the magnificent wide circular staircase to the multiple family gathering rooms, offices, bedrooms and bathrooms, Hattie sold the house with all the furnishings to a buyer who in turn sold it almost immediately to a third party. The house remains under the ownership of this third party. With very little modification to the structure the new owner added a plaque on the entrance gate of the home to notify others that new residents were comfortably settled in. The prominent raised letter plaque on the front gate of 1125 16th Street in Washington D.C. reads: Embassy of the Russian Federation.

In contrast, the facility at 9079 Hampton Blvd, Norfolk, VA does not have the impressive, raised letter plaque at the front gate. It has a more reserved sign that reads, simply, "Naval Station Norfolk." Rather plain, considering it is announcing the largest Naval Station in the world.

On a sunny October morning in 1967, Chief Petty Officer John Anthony Walker pulled his 1964 MG to a stop at the front gate of the Norfolk Naval Station, waved to the security guard stationed in the guard shack, and then drove the 192 miles to the 1125 16th Street address.

The directions to the embassy had been memorized. He had practiced the drive mentally multiple times every day over the past several weeks.

Walker was driving to the Soviet embassy that fall morning with one purpose in mind. He was hoping to sell them United States military secrets. He carried with him a collection of documents that included secret government papers on U.S Submarines and, perhaps more importantly at the time, the following months cryptographic code key list for the top-secret KL-47 encryption machine.

Walkers reasoning for his actions was, for him, quite simple. He was near bankruptcy because of a business venture that had gone wrong, and he needed money.

His goal was to open channels of cooperation with the Soviets to provide them with top secret United States Government information on a regular basis. As it turned out, with the misguided help of the United States Navy, the FBI, and the US government it ultimately became a very lucrative business arrangement for both him and the Soviets.

Chief Petty Officer John Walkers trip to Washington DC that morning was the first leg of a covert relationship he would develop with the Soviets that would continue, unimpeded, for more than 18 years.

His nearly two decades of espionage for the Soviet's would result in the biggest security breech that has ever been perpetrated against the United States of America.

Walker had easy access to top-secret information that he assumed would be valuable to the Soviets. He knew that he could easily provide this information, and he assumed that the Soviets would be willing to pay for it.

His assumptions ultimately proved to be true.

That morning Walker had decided to betray his country – for no other reason than that he was broke.

When he arrived in Washington, he parked his car two blocks

from the Embassy. He pulled the car key from the ignition and held it with whitening fingers. He took several deep breaths, and then, almost absentmindedly, brushed his other hand across the front of his jacket to ensure the documents were still in place.

He got out of the car, locked it, and started walking toward 16th street. His step was quick, his vision tunneled, and his mind focused on his first words to the person inside the embassy. It was at this moment he realized exactly what he was going to attempt to do. He hesitated briefly. It was more of a half step in his stride than a complete hesitation, but it was a half-step that carried him over that line of duty and service to a life of subversion and a title of traitor. He kept moving forward.

He stopped at the front gate and was approached by a guard. Following a brief discussion, the guard stepped back into the guard shack and picked up the phone. After several minutes, the guard hung up the phone, stepped out and told Walker that someone would be out shortly.

Walker watched another guard exit the front door of the embassy and walk toward the guard shack. The two men had a brief discussion, and Walker was asked to follow the man who had just arrived. They walked to the embassy and entered the reception area.

The room was furnished with a leather couch, several chairs and a library table that was occupied by a gentleman wearing a suit. Walker thought that the top of the desk seemed somewhat sparse, holding only a leather desk cover, a phone, a leather binder and a single pen.

Walker was directed to the man at the desk.

"My name is John Walker. I would like to speak to someone in security please."

"Why do you need to see security? Is there a problem?" the man replied. His English was excellent, with only a slight hint of a

Russian accent. This fact seemed to somehow comfort Walker. It provided him with an assurance that he had reached this point, and he was not going to be stopped.

“It is something that I would like to discuss with him.”

The man at the desk ran a reviewing glance at the man standing in front of him. He seemed to sense that Walker was serious, so he picked up the handset and pressed one of the buttons that lined the bottom front of the phone. The button lit and Walker could faintly hear a muffled voice answer in Russian. A conversation in Russian continued for some time before the receptionist hung up the phone and looked up at Walker. “Please take a seat. Someone will be out shortly.”

Presently, a rather large man wearing a double-breasted suit, that seemed more appropriate for a 1940's Humphrey Bogart crime movie, stepped through a door on the right and walked toward the desk. The embassy men spoke, in Russian, for a few moments and then the man turned to Walker and said, “My name is Yakov Lukasevics, I am the Internal Security Specialist at the Embassy. How may I help you?”

Walker stood up and asked if they could possibly go to a more private area to talk.

He moved in front of Walker and raised his arms indicating that he wanted Walker to raise his. “I am sorry, but you can understand our need to ensure the security of our office,” as he patted down Walker looking for weapons. He felt the envelope in Walker’s front jacket pocket and asked him to remove it. Walker reached into his jacket and pulled out the envelope containing the stolen documents. “What is this?” Lukasevics asked.

“It is what I wanted to talk about,” Walker replied.

Seeming satisfied with the answer Lukasevics motioned for Walker to follow him. They walked through the same door that Lukasevics had just entered. The door led to a long hall. Lukasevics walked into the second office on the left of the hall, waited for Walker to enter and then shut the door.

"Please sit-down Mr. Walker."

"Thank you," Walker replied.

"How may I help you?" Lukasevics asked. "We do have a busy schedule, and it might be difficult to make time for you."

Walker began to think that his plan might be crushed before he even had a chance to talk with anyone.

"I have secret information that I would like to discuss."

Without blinking, Lukasevics replied, "And is this information of importance to the Soviet Republic?"

"Yes."

While Lukasevics seemed somewhat aloof and uninterested, he was, in fact, extremely interested. While it was not unusual for walk-ins wanting to sell 'secret' information to appear at the Embassy, most can immediately be uncovered as a plant or a trap. But Lukasevics' initial observation of Walker, even within just the few minutes, told him that this could be something different.

He reached for the phone, pressed a button that lit, and shared a few words with whoever had answered on the other end.

"Won't you please follow me?" He asked Walker. "We can meet in an inside office to discuss your information."

Walker followed Lukasevics through the same door he had entered moments earlier. They walked down a wide, ornate hallway and entered a room with two large sliding doors. Lukasevics pulled the doors apart and entered the room. He motioned Walker to enter the room. "Please, won't you join me," he said.

Lukasevics motioned for Walker to take a seat. "Please make yourself comfortable."

Walker sat in a large leather chair and Lukasevics sat in one directly across from him – no more than three or four feet apart.

"How may I help you?" Lukasevics asked.

Walker, with very little hesitation said, "I can provide you with secret United States government information if you will agree to pay me for it."

Lukasevics, who had years of experience working in intelligence, sensed again that Walker might be someone who could, in fact, be useful to the Soviet Republic. He did question his cavalier attitude, though, and wondered if he was that sure of himself or just stupid. If he were the latter, it would be a mistake to make arrangements of any type with him.

"Please, first, tell me how you were to come upon this 'secret' information."

"I am a Chief Warrant Officer with the United States Navy." Walker replied. "I work with highly classified information on a daily basis. I would like to provide information to you for money." Walker then reached into his jacket pocket and removed the envelope containing the secret stolen documents. He extended the envelope to Lukasevics, but Lukasevics asked him to set it on the desk to his left.

"What is this information you have just laid on the desk?" Lukasevics asked.

"It includes several facsimile copies of top-secret U.S. Submarine sonar advancements and a page of next month's secret key list for the KL-47 cryptographic coding machine. I have brought them today to show you that I am telling the truth."

"What is this KL-47 machine?" Lukasevics asked. "How are

these key lists used?" The questions at this point were somewhat rhetorical, because Lukasevics was fully aware of the names and nomenclature for numerous United States Cryptographic systems.

Anxious to share as much information as possible to hopefully keep Lukasevics' attention, Walker began by telling him that the KL-47 was a secret cryptographic communications machine that is used to decipher encrypted messages that are transmitted to all Naval ships around the world. He went on to share that it worked by using 12 rotors packed in a storage container, and that each rotor had 36 contact points. Eight rotors would be specified by the key list for that day. The other four would be set aside. Each rotor had a movable outside ring that would be rotated manually to a position also defined by the key list.

Lukasevics sat quietly.

Walker continued to share that the key and rotor combinations would change at 0000 Zulu time daily. They would continue using the rotor combinations until the next HJ.

Lukasevics interrupted him, "What is this HJ?"

"HJ stands for Hotel Juliet. It is the time the crypto machine codes are changed for the next day, 0000 Zulu time." Walker, feeling somewhat more comfortable, sensed that he had Lukasevics' attention.

They continued to talk about the crypto machine for fifteen minutes.

The operation of the KL-47 seemed to be well defined in Walker's mind, and it was apparent that, barring a complete hoax, it would be well worth pursuing further discussion with the walk-in. He was impressed with Walker's eidetic overview of the machine – a trait that would prove to be useful in the future. It became obvious that he was not stupid at all, but the 'honesty' in this proposition needed to be further investigated.

Lukasevics excused himself from the room for a moment. He opened and then pulled closed the sliding doors as he left. He was gone for about 10 minutes. Walker felt that the submarine sonar documentation, the crypto code keys, and his review of the machine had been enough to make this meeting a success.

The sliding doors opened and Lukasevics entered followed by the Russian Embassy Station Chief Boris Solomatin. Lukasevics closed the doors again as Solomatin walked toward Walker and extended his hand.

"How do you do Mister Walker. My name is Boris Solomatin. I am the Station Chief at the Embassy and Security Specialist Lukasevics suggested that I spend a few minutes with you to introduce myself and see what we might be able to do to facilitate an agreement between us. You do understand that we must be cautious – both of us. If you don't mind, I would like to ask Specialist Lukasevics to take your code key list to our communications specialists here at the embassy so that they might review its authenticity and relevance to this relationship."

Walker agreed, knowing that if the Soviets had a way to authenticate the code list, they would find it to be real. "Yes, of course, please take the list and examine it." Walker picked up the envelope and handed it to Lukasevics who then left the room.

"Mister Walker," Solomatin began "might I offer you something to drink? Scotch, vodka, bourbon?"

Walker, who by now was feeling pretty sure of himself replied,

"Bourbon, is my go-to drink, thanks."

Lukasevics reviewed the code key list and compared it with copies of similar lists that had come into the hands of the Russian embassy in Japan. It was obvious that they were authentic. The only question now was whether Walker was telling the truth or was it a trap. He returned, with the key list to the room where Walker and Solomatin were talking. He leaned over and whispered something into Solomatin's ear. Solomatin made no indication that what Lukasevics had shared was either positive or negative.

Solomatin thanked the Russian Security Specialist, took the code list, and told Lukasevics that he would be talking with Mr. Walker for a bit longer and that he would catch up with him later. Lukasevics left the room, shutting the door behind him.

Solomatin and Walker continued talking for several hours. Solomatin became confident that Walker was telling the truth, and he realized that this was an unbelievable stroke of luck and perhaps the biggest opportunity that the Soviets had had in years of espionage.

"Can you provide other lists for this machine, Mr. Walker?"

"I can. And I can get information for other crypto machines too."

Solomatin did not inquire about the other machines Walker mentioned. There would be time for that later.

What Walker did not know, and never would, was that the Soviet Embassy in Japan had an embedded spy in the highest levels of the United States naval command in Japan. This Navy spy was in a position to 'persuade' decisions on ship placement and operations for the entire region. At this very time, the Navy in Japan was scheduling the positioning of a spy ship to be located just off the North Korean coast – just beyond the international coastline. The ship, the USS Pueblo, would be completely fitted with top secret cryptographic and radio communications equipment. If Walker could continue to provide cryptographic key lists, the only thing that Russia needed to decipher all American coded naval communications was the actual crypto hardware – the same hardware that would be mounted in the spy ship Pueblo. This was a monumental moment in Russian espionage, and the walk-in, Walker, would become a direct link to the encryption codes for the cryptographic equipment that North Korea would soon capture and provide.

Solomatin had already planned a secure call to Japan to bring them up to date and provide information for their spy in the Naval Command Headquarters.

Solomatin poured himself and Walker another drink and they continued their discussion. He knew that the direction from this point would be to assess how Walker could best be involved to keep him a part of the plan.

While it is extremely unusual for an Embassy Chief to take direct control of handling a walk-in like Walker – it's exactly what he did. It was his task from that point to be the contact, 'friend,' and controller of Walker. He was satisfied that Walker never once mentioned how great the Soviet Republic was during the conversation - a sure tip-off of a trap. Walker was only interested in selling top secret information to the Russians for his own financial benefit. It was a very clean business deal that Solomatin read as a perfect relationship. He told Walker that he would buy information from him. He told him that he would be in touch to explain how the information could be delivered and how the payments would be made.

Solomatin picked up the phone again and spoke briefly. Within minutes a man that Walker had not seen before entered the room and handed Solomatin an envelope. It contained $1,000 American dollars.

The man did not leave the room but stood waiting. Solomatin stood up, followed by Walker. They shook hands and Solomatin handed his new spy the envelope. The relationship was now in place.

Solomatin told Walker that the gentleman would escort him to a car in the Embassy parking area and drive him out of the Embassy so that he would not be seen. Walker followed the man through another door and down a hall to the entrance to the secured embassy parking. They both got in the car and the man drove Walker out and dropped him off two blocks from where his car was parked.

Walker walked to his car, opened the door and got in. He immediately started the engine and headed back to his naval base in Norfolk. He couldn't help but to glance at the rearview mirror to see if he was being followed. He was not. He was once again anxious, but it was overshadowed with the feeling that he was now a spy. He was James Bond. He was so much smarter than all the people at the naval base where he worked. He knew it. And just knowing that made him smile as he drove. He once again briefly ran his hand over his jacket to this time feel an envelope with $1,000 in tens, twenties and fifties. He had made it to the big time.

Solomatin watched Walker leave the meeting room. He then walked to his office, picked up a phone and told the man in the communications center that he wanted to make a secure call to the Soviet Embassy in Japan. He listened for a few seconds and then pressed a red button labeled secure. He began talking. It was a much longer call than normal.

The Embassy in Japan immediately set up a meeting with their inside contact, a United States Naval Officer based in Japan. Their master plan was in place. They would soon have access to most United States Naval top secret encrypted communications.

CHAPTER 4

November 14, Tuesday evening, Spencer's apartment

The shrill ring of the phone startled Spencer. He glanced at his watch and then turned his attention to the phone on the table next to him.

Knowing that the men he had met in Carson's office that morning would be having him followed until he left for Hawaii, he had to assume that his phone had been tapped. He questioned if he should answer it. He wanted to avoid inadvertently bringing anyone else under suspicion; especially the one person he suspected was on the other end of the line.

The phone continued ringing.

"Dammit!"

He picked up the handset, brought it slowly to his ear and said, "Hello."

An obviously inebriated young woman said, "Hi it's me. I'm getting married! Yep, today's the day Bill finally asked me. And of course, you are going to be my bride's maid. Can't talk now. Call me tomorrow, but not too early.". After what sounded like several attempts to put the hand set back on the switch hook the line went dead.

Sheila's coded message had been received.

During their first collaboration, when they decided to bypass filing certain paper trails to keep Mark Williams at bay, they also developed a simple, secure way to talk privately between themselves outside the constricts of the bureau. When either one of them used the code phrase "Today's the day," Spencer would find a public phone, and at exactly 19:00 hours a pay phone in a small deli, near Sheila's apartment would ring. Sheila would be there to answer the phone.

Spencer glanced again at the clock. It was 18:48. He didn't have much time.

Placing the handset back on the phone, he got up and walked toward his bedroom, pausing briefly to turn on the stereo. His bedroom was dark. He walked to the window, pulled the curtain back slightly and peeked out. A black Ford sedan was parked directly across from his second-floor apartment, and he could just make out the profiles of two men setting in the front seat. The steamed windshield hinted that they had been settled for some time.

Knowing that he could be seen through the shear covered windows behind his recliner, he walked back into the living room and stood next to it. He picked up the half bottle of Dewar's and the glass that were still setting on the table from the night before, and somewhat theatrically poured a drink. He then sat down. He would have to assume that the two men in the black Ford outside his apartment would have seen him. He continued to sit quietly.

"They will stop at nothing to make this go away James; absolutely nothing."

Sidwell's foreboding warning had been living, rent free, deep in his subconscious only to keep surfacing at the least opportune times. He brushed aside the thought and focused on how he was going to get out of the chair unnoticed and then out of the apartment. He raised his hand slightly to briefly grasp the handle of his shoulder holstered Smith & Wesson. It seemed an appropriate thing to do at the time.

He pulled himself out of the chair and remained crouched until he was out of sight of the window. He then stood up and grabbed his jacket and keys. The lights and stereo were still on as he walked out the apartment door into the hallway. He took the back stairway and exited in the rear of the building where a small parking lot led to the road running parallel to his. He walked several blocks to a group of three empty phone booths and entered the middle booth.

At exactly 7:00 PM the phone in the small deli in Washington began to ring. Sheila picked up the handset before the second ring.

"Hello."

Spencer responded, "Can we meet?"

"Italian sounds perfect. Seven thirty." she replied. They hung up.

The Italian restaurant they were headed to was one of four predefined locations for clandestine meetings to discuss matters that needed to be kept from the Bureau – or certain members of the Bureau.

They had frequented all of them during their years of work together. As their relationship grew, they oftentimes extended these work meetings to spend time on more personal matters. They found it gave them a much-needed opportunity to step away from the day-to-day pressure of their jobs, and it also gave them more time to just be together.

Spencer arrived several minutes before Sheila. He waited just inside the front door out of sight of any passerby.

Sheila walked in and stopped momentarily, looking for him.

"Sheila." James said softly.

She turned her head in the direction of his voice and saw him standing to her left. She stepped toward him and embraced him tightly. He immediately recognized her favorite perfume, Evening in Paris. She smelled of violet and rose and vanilla and sandalwood. She smelled lovely. With her arms around him he could sense the warmth of her body even from beneath the heavy jacket she was wearing.

She finally pulled away, now feeling embarrassed by the unsolicited, extended embrace. She felt the warmth in her cheeks as she stood next to him.

"Hello James." She said somewhat sheepishly.

"Hello Sheila." He responded with a slight grin.

A young waitress stepped forward and thankfully interrupted the somewhat awkward moment, "Good evening," she said with a welcoming smile. "Would you prefer a table or booth?"

Spencer pointed to a booth to the left, away from the windows, and asked if it was available. There were no diners nearby and it seemed to be a safe place to talk.

"Of course," she replied as the three of them walked it its direction.

They sat down and the waitress handed them both a menu.

"May I get you something to drink?"

James looked at Sheila. "What would you like?"

"I'll have what you're having tonight, James." Sheila would normally have asked for a Cabernet Sauvignon but tonight seemed better suited to something stronger.

"May we please have two Dewar's with just a splash of water?" He looked again at Sheila and asked, "Ice?"

"No ice," she replied. She knew that James never had ice with his scotch. He once told her that he could never understand why anyone would add ice to a blended whisky. Ice would slowly dilute the essence of the perfect balance of the blended single malts that were highlighted by the light splash of water. She wasn't sure she understood exactly what he meant, but he liked his scotch with no ice and that's how she would have hers.

He turned again to the waitress smiling and said "That would be no ice in either. Thanks."

She left and Sheila turned back to James, a concerned look on her face. She then spoke quietly.

"This is your last day at the Washington Field Office, and you are transferring to Hawaii. What the hell is going on James?"

"I'm not going to ask how you know that" he replied with a smile. But the smile faded quickly.

"Today Carson gave me the option to retire from the Bureau or move to Hawaii on Saturday."

Sheila almost yelled, "What? What the hell happened?" She immediately looked around to see if anyone had overheard her.

"Sheila, I really don't want to involve you in any of this."

"You've been told to leave the bureau or move to Hawaii on Saturday, and you just don't want me involved in any of this? What 'this' are you talking about James?"

"If anyone finds out you know what happened over the past couple of days, Sheila, you will be in immediate danger."

"James, we both work for an organization that can put us in danger at any time. That's why we get paid the big bucks." Her lips slowly formed one of her lovely smiles as she looked at him. "I'm a big girl James. I'll take that chance."

Just then the waitress returned with the drinks. "Have you had a chance to decide on your meal, or could you use a few more minutes?"

Sheila looked at James and asked, "How's a pepperoni and mushroom pizza sound?"

"Perfect."

Sheila turned back to the girl and said "Then we'll have one medium pepperoni and mushroom pizza. Oh, can you add extra cheese too please?"

The waitress acknowledged their order, smiled, and walked away.

They both took a sip of their scotch. Sheila grimaced slightly with her first sip. It certainly wasn't a Cabernet. She looked at Spencer with focused eyes, "OK James, tell me what the hell is going on."

Spencer pursed his lips and brought his hand to his chin. He was torn between sharing the information, concerned for her safety, and his belief that she deserved to know the truth; he decided to tell her everything from the beginning.

He first told her about the envelope in his coat pocket, the Top-Secret MI6 intelligence report, the phone call, and then the meeting at the Tune Inn.

Spencer stopped talking when the waitress returned with their meal. She placed the wooden tray with the steaming pizza on the table along with two plates and then pulled two napkin-wrapped silverware sets from her apron and set them next to the plates.

"Can I get you anything else?"

Spencer looked at the near empty glasses of scotch and asked

Sheila if she would like another.

Sheila responded immediately, "I think another round of drinks would be perfect."

They sat quietly waiting for the waitress to return with the two glasses of Dewar's. Spencer took the opportunity to put a slice of the still sizzling pizza on each plate. Once the drinks were delivered, Spencer continued the story.

He told her about the navy spy in Norfolk, the murder of Sidwell, the meeting with the two men in Carson's office, and his option to either resign or move to Hawaii. She sat quietly, never interrupting, never glancing away.

When he finally finished, Sheila remained quiet.

He understood that Sheila's calm, silent demeanor juxtaposed with the logical brilliance of a highly skilled mind that was working at warp speed to make sense of the story she had just heard.

Her eyes moved to the glass of Whisky sitting in front of her. She then looked up at James again, smiled, and said, "Why don't you ever just focus on the easy cases, it would really make things so much simpler – for both of us."

Sheila always had the perfect way to break the tension when it was important that the tension was broken. They both smiled.

"OK, I have some questions." she said.

"I thought you might," James replied while reaching for his scotch.

They talked together in the private booth in the restaurant for the next two hours.

James and Sheila were both completely aware of the complex ramifications of the story he had just shared. The blatant cover-up by the FBI deeply undermined the belief they each had for the integrity of the bureau. Oh, it's not that they were naive enough to think that the bureau hadn't ever crossed the line before to make their case. In fact, sometimes it seemed that there wasn't even a line in place for them to worry about crossing. But this was bigger – much bigger. The bureau was involved in a cover-up that could affect the security of the United States. And it involved the very top echelon of leadership at the FBI, the United States Navy, and the federal government.

They also clearly understood that they were on their own with this information, and if any of this conversation became known to others, their lives would be at risk. The irony didn't escape either of them. The organization that they had both devoted their careers to would easily have them both killed for just doing their job.

"James, is there any way we can stop this spy in Norfolk?"

"I don't see how we can, Sheila. We have absolutely no one to pass on this information – and there is no way you're getting involved on your own. You realize that if we were to continue with this in any way, and were discovered, we would be flagged as rogue – not a moniker that suggests a long life."

He paused for a few moments, and then continued, "Before, we would have had the backing of the WFO, but that isn't the case now. The bastards are moving me to Hawaii next week. Their plan is to get me out of the way, and transferring me five thousand miles across the globe pretty much does that. I hate to say it, but this time, we just have to walk away.

Sheila responded, "This is bull shit."

Spencer, sensing that she might start thinking of doing something herself, repeated, "And, again, there is absolutely no way that you are going to get involved. We have no back-up, and this is way too dangerous."

They both took a sip of scotch and placed their glasses back on the table.

“How bad do you think this can all turn out if this spy in Norfolk isn’t stopped?” Sheila inquired.

“Selling top secret cryptographic code key lists to the Soviets is about as bad as it gets.”

“This is big James. This is so totally fucked up.”

James nodded his head as he replied, “The FBI, the Navy, the federal government, even SIS want to make this all just disappear because it would be an inconvenience to some important people. These are the same people we report to Sheila! You know, the past two days have undermined everything I admired about this job. I feel like I’ve been used since the day I signed up. And the bureau is making sure there isn’t a damn thing we can do to stop this son-of-a-bitch from handing over top-secret information to the Soviets. You’re right Sheila, this is totally fucked up.”

“James, I don’t know how I can possibly continue working for them. What about you?”

“Right now, Sheila, I would love to walk away, but unfortunately, I have a pension to think about. I’d rather not be pumping gas at the corner Esso station until my retirement benefits start rolling in.” James looked into Sheila’s eyes and smiled softly.

“That makes two of us,” she responded. “But there has to be some way out of this nightmare.”

“What do you say we find a little Esso station somewhere and pump gas together?” he asked, with a grin.

“Just say the word!” She responded with a huge smile.

“Honestly, James, you know I haven’t been happy at the bureau for years. There’s nothing keeping me here, especially now.”

“How many promotions have you been passed over that should

have been yours," he asked.

"I know. Oh, the first few years were new and exciting," she continued, "but it became obvious that no matter how good I was at my job, there was no way I would ever be put up for advancement – real advancement. I'm being used every day, and I know it. After these revelations, and with you being transferred, I'm going to start looking. I need something new."

Spencer sat quietly, he looked sad.

"How about this, James. You give me a state where you'd like to call home, and I'll find a quiet little town with a quiet little Esso station that we can run away together to and pump gas. You know, I do research kind of things for a living, so I could have everything in place by noon tomorrow." Her smile was soft and warm.

The words "we can run away together to" caught James's attention. He was never one to show emotions, but he had been through hell the past couple of days and was about to be pulled away from the one person who meant more to him than anyone. He swallowed deeply.

"Why have you stayed on as long as you have?" he asked.

"Honestly James, the only reason I have stayed as long as I have is because I knew you would be there every morning."

Sheila lowered her head, and James could see that she was crying. "I just can't lose you."

James reached across the table and grasped her hand softly.

"I don't know why I just told you that James, I am so sorry," she sobbed.

He gently lifted his hand to her cheek and said, "Sheila, I can't lose you either."

They sat quietly in the booth, both understanding the

complexities of their lives, their careers, and the relationship they had developed.

"Sheila, you are brilliant and beautiful, and warm and caring and funny. And there is no one I'd rather spend my time, all my time, with." His comforting grin softened the moment.

Sheila always loved that grin.

James continued, "I am being moved thousands of miles away and I am finally telling you how I have always felt about you. Feel free to call me an idiot at any time here."

"You? I'm the idiot. You have no idea how many times I've watched Casablanca and pictured us as Rick and Ilsa. I know stupid right? The story always ends with us standing in the mist at an obscure airport, but in my version, I am not getting on the plane and leaving you. We are getting on the plane together to fly away from, well, everything. James, the only reason I haven't found another job is because I knew you would be there every day."

Sheila stopped for a moment and softly dabbed her eyes with her napkin.

"Oh my god, I don't know why I am telling you all this James. I don't do things like that. Maybe it's because I will be totally devastated when you leave, and I'm hoping if I just keep blabbering on long enough you won't go. Or maybe it's that second glass of Dewar's talking."

"In that case, I'm glad we didn't stop at one." Spencer replied with that warm smile again.

"What can we do James?"

"Sheila, you may think this is totally crazy, but what would you think about moving to Hawaii with me when this settles down and we can start all over. We can get a apartment or a house and actually do things like go out on real dates and talk about things other than work – or, if you like, we can just sit in a car under a palm tree and spy on people walking by. We could easily live on my new salary."

She looked lovingly into his eyes and said, "I don't see anything crazy about that at all."

They sat quietly for a few moments still drawn into each other's eyes.

Sheila lifted her glass as if she was going to make a toast; James lifted his.

"Here's to setting in a car under a palm tree and spying on people," she said. They both laughed and tapped their glasses together.

"James, I can't think of any reason we couldn't make it happen. Oh, we would obviously have to be extremely cautious, but that we can handle. Will you promise me, though, that we can be together as soon as we possibly can. You have no idea how much I am going to miss you."

Spencer hesitated for a second. reached over the table again and put his hands over hers again, softly clasping them.

"In all honesty, Sheila, things should settle down and be forgotten within a couple of months. Once I'm out of the picture, everyone will back off. Can you hold on until then?"

Sheila thought for a second and said, "That could be perfect. It will give you time to settle into your new position and find an apartment, and it will give me time to close things up on this end. And it will be enough time to avoid raising any suspicion."

She smiled and continued, "I can't believe we are talking about having our whole future to plan together." And then she started laughing and said, "And it only took you being shipped off five thousand miles away for us to finally figure this out."

It was then that the waitress stopped at the table.

"I hope everything was OK." She said smiling, as she handed James the bill.

Sheila and James both responded that everything was just perfect. James pulled his wallet from his back pocket, counted out the money and handed it to the young girl.

"Oh, I hope we didn't keep you too late." Sheila said.

"No, no it wasn't a problem at all, I still have another half hour. Thank you both so much and have a nice evening." She smiled, turned and walked away.

"Well, Miss Anderson, it sounds like we have some planning to do. What do you say we get out of here and start?"

When they stood up, Spencer helped Sheila with her coat and then took her hand as they walked out of the restaurant.

He laughed and said, "I guess I should have asked how you got here this evening."

"I took a cab," she answered, "because I wasn't sure if I would be in any condition to drive home. Do you have your car?"

"No, I took a cab too. We obviously were thinking the same thing. We'll share one if that's ok."

"Of course," she quickly replied.

They stepped to the curb and Spencer waved down a cab. When the driver asked where they were going, Sheila gave her address. They sat in the cab quietly, still holding hands. Spencer again was aware of the soft hint of violet and rose and vanilla and sandalwood. He hoped the ride would never end.

The cab came to a stop in front of Sheila's apartment. She turned to Spencer and looked softly into his eyes. "I don't think I want to be alone tonight, James."

They both got out of the cab and walked to the door of her apartment building. She removed her purse from her shoulder. "Let me get my keys. I know they're in here somewhere." She laughed and said, "I could probably find them faster if I hadn't had that last drink."

"And this is exactly why we needed to get a cab," Spencer laughed.

They walked into her apartment, and Sheila turned on the light in the entrance hall, closed the door and locked it. As they stepped into the living room, she told James to just throw his coat over the back of the couch. Sheila laid her purse on the end table, tossed her coat on top of his, and then moved close to Spencer. He pulled her to him and their lips met. As they pulled apart, Sheila said, with a smile, "And we can still sit in the car under a palm tree and spy on people, right? I mean you did promise."

He gave her a gentle kiss, smiled and said, "I promise. Every night."

The next morning.

James glanced at the clock on Sheila's nightstand. It was 5:15 AM. He realized the night couldn't have been more perfect as he returned his gaze to her beautiful face, which was softly highlighted by the muted glow of the streetlights shining through the sheer curtains on the bedroom window. Sheila was lying on her side, her knees pulled up snugly, her arms crossed gently in front of her.

Sheila's eyes opened. She looked at James and asked, "Why did you spend the night?"

"What? I thought you wanted me to spend the night?"

"No, no, I did want you to spend the night, James. But why did you spend the night now?"

"OK, I'm confused," James responded.

"I mean we have known each other and worked closely together six years. We have both been single that entire time, and I know for a fact that over those six years you mentioned exactly three times that I was pretty and three times that I smelled wonderful. Those were your words - you smell wonderful – three times. Now how could I not have succumbed to such obvious and consistent wooing? Just why didn't we spend the night together years ago?"

Spencer chuckled and smiled. "So, your sharp wit isn't something that you develop and nurture during the day? You wake up at 5:20 in the morning and you are ready to take on all comers."

"Hey, that's just me," she said, returning his smile.

James pulled himself up in bed, propped up the pillow and leaned against the headboard.

"Sheila," he said, "I have dreamed of spending an evening – every evening – with you. I just got sucked up in the damn craziness of the job, we both did, and somehow lost sight of what's important in life." He hesitated for a few seconds, smiled, and said, "But that all changes. We will soon be living a wonderful, quiet life together on a beautiful island."

She rubbed his arm softly and said, "We both just needed more time, James. And now we don't."

"They aren't going to beat us on this Sheila. No matter what happens, when all is said and done, we are going to be the ones who come out on top."

Sheila smiled and said, "I like the way you think James."

He pulled her to him, and they embraced warmly. Unfortunately, the alarm clock began buzzing at exactly 5:30 and they had to pull apart and begin the day. But this day was different. It was the first day of what was going to be a wonderful life together.

He dressed quickly and they hugged one final time at the door before he left. She kissed him softly, smiled, and said, "We have some planning to do."

He smiled and said, "A short-term, long-distance romance is something we can get through." And then he said, "I love you, Sheila."

She leaned in and kissed him warmly again. "I love you too, James."

Spencer stepped from the cab in the parking lot behind his apartment. He entered the rear door of his building and climbed the three flights of stairs. Quietly unlocking his apartment door and stepping in, he remained out of the sight of the living room windows as he removed his coat and hung it on the rack and then crouched down to make his way to the recliner. He pulled himself into it without being seen from the front windows. He then stood up - the apartment light still casting a shadow on the curtains - and stretched several times before walking to his bedroom. Pulling the bedroom curtain aside slightly he could see that the car with the two men was still setting where it had been when he left the apartment the night before.

CHAPTER 5

Monday, November 20, 1967
Honolulu Hawaii FBI Field Office

Arrival in Honolulu

Newly arrived and promoted James Spencer stepped from the cab in front of 735 Bishop Street. The temperature was 76 degrees. The sun was shining brightly and a gentle, warm breeze with a light hint of Plumeria blossoms welcomed him to his new place of business.

As the cab pulled away, he stood for a moment taking in his new surroundings. His thoughts jumped back to just one week earlier, when his morning began with torrential rains and cold gusty wind in Washington DC. Today was beginning a new chapter in paradise. Or so it seemed.

He braced himself for the day ahead and walked across the sidewalk to the arched portals opening to the covered entrance. He opened the door and walked into a somewhat surprisingly handsome gold dominated Art Deco designed entrance lobby defined by beautiful marble and bricks. A large plaque to his right shared that he was in the lobby of the "Dillingham Transportation Building built in 1929". He walked across the now defined and dated lobby to the elevators and perused the company tenant list for a room number. His eyes scrolled down to FBI - 301. He pressed the up button and was a bit surprised that the door directly in front of him opened so quickly. He stepped into the elevator and pressed 3. The button lit and a bell dinged.

As the door closed, he steeled himself for the upcoming day. His thoughts drifted briefly to a future with Sheila, but that would have to come later.

A bell dinged again as the elevator came to a stop. The door opened. He stepped out, glanced at the arrow pointing to Rooms 300-310, turned to his left and walked down the hall.

FBI Special Agent in Charge James Spencer was beginning his first day of work in his new position in Honolulu, Hawaii. As an outsider being moved into a lead position that would normally have been filled internally, his expectations of being well received by his new team were extremely low.

Room 301 was at the end of the hall. The smoked glass window on the door provided the background for the somewhat ominous black lettering that read Federal Bureau of Investigation. Spencer hesitated for a moment and then opened the door and walked in. The room was an open area corner room with windows on two walls and an array of desks, chairs, and filing cabinets. Two closed doors to what he guessed were offices were to the right. Several of the windows were open and a light breeze encircled the open area.

The desk closest to the hall door was occupied by a smartly dressed blonde-haired woman, who appeared to be in her thirties. She was on the phone and, seeing Spencer, raised a finger to indicate she was finishing up. He noticed two men, both on the phone, at other desks. It was apparent from their animated voices and movements that they would be on for a while. He waited. The woman completed the call, quickly finished her notes and stood to greet the man who she suspected to be the new boss.

“Good morning. I'm Jim Spencer.”

“She held out her hand, smiled and said, “Good morning, sir, I'm Agent Coleman, Iris Coleman.”

Spencer shook her hand and replied, “Good morning, Agent Coleman.”

She continued, “We were only notified on Thursday that you would be arriving today, so I apologize that we aren't as organized for your arrival as we should be. Your office is the one closest to the window on the right over there. She pointed and added that, “We haven't cleaned it out since Agent Wilson was last in it, well, just about two weeks ago.”

“No, no, that's alright. I understand.” Spencer responded. “I was so sorry to hear about that tragic accident. I was told that Agent Wilson was well respected and liked by everyone in your office.”

Iris responded quietly, “He was.”

“I realize that my move into his position, especially under these circumstances, is going to be difficult for all of us for a while. I wish things could have been more structured and coordinated. I do apologize for the position this has put you all in.”

“I understand how these things can sometimes work, Sir. I’m sure we will all get through it in time.”

Spencer smiled and nodded his head.

“I see that both of the other agents are on their phones, so why don’t I show you to your office to get settled in.”

“Sounds like a great idea Agent Coleman.” Spencer replied.

As they walked toward Spencer’s new office, Coleman continued.

"We only have one key for the door. Mike, sorry, Agent Wilson, had his key with him when he..." Her voice faded off. "And I haven't had a copy made yet. Here, let me get it open for you so you can relax for a second until they are freed up. It's been locked since he left that Friday. Alice, his wife, said that she would be in to collect all his personal items as soon as she got back from the states. They held a memorial service in his hometown in Oklahoma last week, and she was staying on to find a place to live. She was also from Oklahoma, and I understand that she is planning to move back to be close to family."

She paused for a moment and then said, "We can try to get in today and get all of his personal..."

"No, no that's fine Agent Coleman," Spencer interrupted. "Let me sit down for a couple of minutes and get organized as best I can. We can arrange to pick up Agent Wilson's personal items a bit later." Spencer's response was sensitive to her feelings, but he also was searching for a few quiet minutes to try and gather his thoughts. His very fast transfer from special Agent in the Washington D.C. Bureau to an island 5000 miles away still hadn't been resolved in his mind.

Iris opened the door to a dark office and switched on the light. "It is a little warm in here," she commented. "The overhead fan helps, but it sometimes just moves the hot air around. You might want to open your window. There's usually a nice breeze coming off the ocean at this time of the day, and it really makes a difference."

"Thanks, that's exactly what I am going to do," he responded.

Coleman turned to walk back to her desk. "Would you like me to close your door sir?"

"No, you can just leave it open, thanks."

She stopped and said, "Oh, here is the key sir." Spencer reached for it and thanked her again.

As she walked away, he stepped behind the desk, sat his briefcase on the floor next to the chair and then focused on opening the window. A set of wooden Venetian blinds were closed and stretched from the top of the window to the sill. He pulled the draw cord and raised them halfway. He noticed that the paint on the window frame was chipped and there were areas of caulking missing around the glass. Guessing that he was going to have to fight with the window to raise it, he wished now that he had asked Iris to close the door so no one would see him wresting with it. But to his surprise it slid up easily. A refreshing breeze immediately filled the room. The leaves of a tall palm tree directly outside his window were waving quietly in the gentle gusts.

He sat down at his new desk and thought, "Where to begin?" With a quick glance around the office, he noticed several pictures that Agent Wilson had hanging on the walls. There were pictures of his family, and a few pictures that appeared to have been taken at business meetings. There was one picture on the wall next to the door, though, that seemed different and somewhat out of place. While all the other pictures were well structured and in color, the one on the wall by the door was a simply framed, black and white snapshot.

Spencer had always been sensitive to things that seemed out of place. It was probably one of the traits that made him an excellent agent. He glanced at the other pictures again and then back to the black and white snapshot. It didn't feel right – he wasn't sure why – but it didn't. He got up from the desk, walked to the black framed photograph and removed it from the wall.

He sat down again holding the picture in his hands and leaned back in his chair. It was a picture of a group of men gathered on what he guessed was a chartered fishing boat. He recognized one of the men to be Agent Wilson from his other pictures on his walls in his office. Each had a bottle of beer held high as if toasting something, or someone. The seven men all seemed to be in good spirits. He thought that perhaps the beer had something to do with that.

The photo, which was a rather poor snapshot, had one of the men's head cut off. The beer labels that were visible in the men's hands were all Heineken. He also noticed the headless man in the picture was wearing a polo shirt with a Heineken logo. Spencer guessed this to be the provider of the liquid refreshments for the fishing trip.

It didn't escape him that his predecessor had died on a chartered fishing boat.

He pulled open the top drawer on the right side of his desk and put the picture in the drawer. It wouldn't be in the box of personal items going to his wife. Spencer wasn't sure why he kept the picture. As far as he knew, Wilson's death was nothing more than an unfortunate accident. But he had learned over the years not to question these triggered responses to things that seemed out of place. He surmised that the photo might be of some importance, but he really had no idea why. None the less, he closed the drawer with the photo in it.

Glancing up he noticed that the two men in the front office were off their phones, so he got up and walked into the open office area.

"Good morning, I'm Jim Spencer and I just wanted to take a second to say hello and introduce myself. This transfer was rushed, for all of us, and I'm afraid I didn't have an opportunity to get caught up on names and positions."

Spencer stepped forward and reached out to shake the hand of a very large man with an obvious Hawaiian ancestry. "Hi."

The man stood to meet Spencer, smiled, and said, "Hi, I'm Agent Tim Kamaka. Nice to meet you, and welcome." Spencer looked up and guessed him to be at least six foot five. From the fit of his shirt Spencer also guessed that Kamaka probably spent a lot of time at the gym lifting weights – heavy weights. His formidable body cast a shadow as he stood and reached out to shake Spencer's hand.

His hand was huge, but his handshake was gentle. Tim had a comfortable, honest smile. Spencer liked him immediately. As he shook his hand, he couldn't help but notice how small the shoulder holstered Smith and Wesson seemed against his large frame.

"It's nice to meet you Agent Kamaka, and thanks." Spencer thought that Tim was someone he would want on his side in a fight.

He then turned to a shorter, balding man with a scowl that seemed etched as a permanent fixture on his face. He reminded you of that guy you saw coming down the isle of the plane, and you prayed to God that he wasn't looking for the empty seat next to you. Spencer immediately ascertained that this probably wasn't the team player who showed up with donuts in the morning to share with his co-workers.

"Hello."

With a gesture that was meant to show his displeasure of having to welcome his new superior, the man reached out his hand, without standing, and said "I'm Agent Shuff, hope Honolulu is to your liking."

Spencer was going to say it was certainly a change from Washington D.C. but thought the reference to being from outside the department wouldn't have been a particularly smart way to start the conversation.

"Hawaii is certainly beautiful. Nice to meet you, Agent Shuff."

"How did you end up getting moved from Washington D.C.?"

Shuff asked. "Kind of a step down, isn't it?"

The sarcastic tone of the question immediately irked Spencer, but he withheld sharing his first thoughts.

"Artistic differences with my boss in Washington," Spencer replied and ended the conversation by turning away from Shuff and walking toward Agent Coleman. He reached out and shook her hand and said, "Hello again Agent Coleman." Coleman smiled in a bit more relaxed manner and said "Hello again. Welcome to Hawaii."

Spencer observed that two of the other three desks were cluttered and the third was obviously unused.

"Two people out of the office right now?"

"Yes sir." She pointed to the desk closest to them. "Agent Vince, Steve Vince is at the main police station here in Honolulu acting as FBI liaison to a drug smuggling operation that they are close to busting. And Agent William Tapper sits at that desk next to Agent Kamaka. He's been on Guam and Rota for the past week finishing up the paperwork on the boating accident."

"Rota?"

"Oh, sorry, Sir, that is an island north of Guam. It's where the fishing boat was chartered. The boat that Agent Wilson was on when – well, the one that exploded. We do have one agent stationed in Guam, Agent John Neuser, and Agent Tapper is working with him."

Spencer was acutely aware that his knowledge of the area under his jurisdiction was extremely limited, and it only highlighted his 'outside' credentials. This is not how transfers are handled in the Bureau, especially for agents taking over a command position.

"Thanks, Agent Coleman."

He then turned to include the two men and said, "I don't want to interrupt all of you now, but if you could each put together a short overview of the cases you are working on when you have some time, I would appreciate it. We can get together after lunch tomorrow, starting about 1:30, to go over them. It shouldn't take more than a half hour each. You don't have to go into depth on the overview, just some quick notes to help get me orientated."

Shuff mumbled an acerbic comment under his breath.

"Is there a problem Agent Shuff?"

Spencer's immediate, sharp tone startled Shuff, which is exactly what he had intended. Not waiting for Shuff to respond, he continued.

"Nice meeting you all, and if you have any questions, I'd be happy to answer anything I can. I know I'll have plenty of questions for you."

Coleman and Kamaka both smiled and nodded. Shuff turned away and didn't bother acknowledging the statement. Spencer walked back to his office and shut the door.

As he entered the room, he noticed a binder that was labeled 'Procedure Manual' setting on a top shelf of one of the bookcases. He stopped and removed it as he walked by and sat it on his desk. Spencer was fully aware of bureau procedures in Washington D.C., but he was now in Hawaii, and it would make sense to review the directives for any differences. It sounded like as good a place as any to start. He opened the binder and began reading.

As he spent the next few hours covering the manual, it occurred to him that even though he had traveled to an island five thousand miles from Washington D.C., the multiple threats the FBI was faced with every day and the numerous bad players involved hadn't changed. Corrupt people were doing the same bad things no matter where you were.

Just then a tap on the door pulled him from his reading.

Agent Coleman leaned in around the door frame and said: “Sir, Tim and I are running out to grab a hamburger. Can we bring you something back? There's a sandwich shop just around the corner on Queen Street, and they are known for their hamburgers. Well, at least we all like them,” she said, smiling. And then to close the sale, she said, “And they’re quick.”

Spencer glanced at his watch, “Wow, I had no idea it was after noon already. Sure, I'd appreciate you grabbing me a cheeseburger and a Coke or Pepsi? Oh, and a small order of fries if they have them."

“They do and we will. Be right back.”

Spencer reached for his wallet to give Coleman some money, but she said she would bring back a receipt, and he could pay her then.

In less than 15 minutes Coleman knocked on the door frame again and said, “Sir, here is your lunch.” She reached over his desk to hand him a bag and about six paper napkins. She noticed his look when he saw the bunch of napkins and she said with a laugh, “You'll probably need all of them.” She sat the Coke on his desk.

“Thanks. Wow, they really are quick,” Spencer replied. He took the brown, grease-stained bag and napkins. He took about half of the napkins and sat them on his desk and placed the bag on them. He took a small bag of fries out of the bigger bag and sat it on his desk.

Coleman was looking through the receipts as she responded. “That's one of the reasons we like it. It's kind of our go to place. Probably shouldn't be because we laugh about it is adding a pound to our weight every time we stop in, but you can't beat that fast service and the food.”

“Here's your bill. Wait, that's Tim's, you don't want that one. He isn't a light eater.”

Spencer paid Coleman for lunch and thanked her again.

As Coleman was taking the money, she smiled and said, “They probably aren’t the best lunch food choice, and they will probably kill you, but we’ve all decided they’re worth the risk.” She walked out of the room, closing the door behind her.

Spencer pulled the cheeseburger out of the bag. The paper wrapper was drenched in grease. He grabbed another napkin, added it to the grease drenched paper wrapper on the cheeseburger, opened it and took a bite.

He immediately realized why this was one of their favorite lunch spots. It was delicious.

He finished the hamburger and fries, wiped his hands with the remainder of the napkins and then walked to the men’s room to wash his hands. He was going to share how good the cheeseburger was, but everyone was on the phone. When he got back to his office, he continued reading the manual. The afternoon went by quickly. Iris and Tim were still at their desks when he pulled his office door closed and locked it.

“I’m headed out guys,” he said smiling. “Oh, and the next time you run out for hamburgers, count me in. They really are worth an early death.” Coleman and Kamaka both laughed and said good night.

On the elevator ride to the lobby, his thoughts returned to Sheila and finding a place for them both on the island to settle down; perhaps this just could be the perfect, quiet spot to finish his career after all.

CHAPTER 6

Tuesday morning, November 21, 1967

Spencer sat in his office chair holding a dark blue coffee mug that was emblazoned with the word SPAM in yellow lettering. It was one of the random mugs he had happened to pick up at the office coffee table that morning. He wasn't particularly excited about the logo, but he did like the feel of it; the weight and the way it fit his hand. A good coffee mug must have the right feel. He thought he just might lay claim to it for his personal use while he was there.

He took a sip of what was surprisingly good coffee, leaned back in his chair and appraised his new office. It was, he felt, somewhat sparsely furnished. Two uncomfortable looking wooden chairs sat in front of his desk, and two waist high metal bookcases lined the wall to his left. He was impressed, though, that all of the shelves of the bookcases were neatly organized with binders of varying widths and colors.

He then noticed a small wooden table next to the bookcases that held an old Zenith radio. The radio had a wooden case with a cloth covered speaker on the front left and a large dial with three round knobs on the right. He wasn't sure how he had missed it when he was in the office the day before. Spencer sat his newly claimed SPAM coffee mug on the desk and got up to take a closer look. Wondering if it still worked, he turned the on/off knob. The dial lit up, and the radio started to come to life. After several seconds of static, while the vacuum tubes were heating up, he stood listening to the last twenty seconds of Helen Forrest singing '*Someone to watch over me*'. The radio was surprisingly clear.

The music ended and an announcer broke the silence. "This is KGMB, Honolulu, Hawaii."

A catchy jingle that began with the sound of coconuts being knocked together was followed by an announcement: 'It's the Coconut Wireless News!'

Spencer remained listening as a disc jockey named Akuhead Pupule shared the highlights of the past day along with some comments about the mayor, local sports, the traffic – and a bank that was giving away one-hundred-dollar bills to the first fifty people who showed up that morning. The guy was obviously the go-to morning show personality in Honolulu. Spencer turned down the volume and left the radio on.

In 1967, the disc jockey Spencer happened across on the radio that morning, Akuhead Pupule (Hal Lewis), was a legend in Honolulu and was said to be the highest paid disc jockey in America.

He returned to his desk and sat down. Looking for current personnel activity files, he logically pulled out the large file drawer on the right side. He took notice that all the files in the drawer had neatly typed color-coded labels; were compiled alphabetically by each of the agent's names and seemed to be equally spaced. He reflected that his own desk files had never been as organized. He was beginning to learn a little about his predecessor.

Spencer thought that the first file, Coleman, was as good a place as any to begin. He removed the file, laid it on top of his desk and began reading. He continued perusing all the documents in Coleman's file and returned it to the drawer. The next neatly tabbed and labeled file was for Kamaka. He pulled it out and sat it on his desk.

It was just then that several light taps on the door caught his attention. He looked up. It was Kamaka. Spencer waved him in.

Tim opened the door and took a small step into Spencer's office. "Hey, you're already an islander if you're listening to Aku. He's the man."

"Aku?" Spencer questioned. "Oh, the radio. I forgot I had that on."

"He's the only guy to listen to in the morning! The man is crazy," Kamaka said smiling.

"I'm gathering that," Spencer replied, also smiling.

"Sorry Sir, I didn't mean to interrupt you like that, but we just got a call from Tapper, and he said they will be getting the Medical Examiners report in the next couple of days, and he was going to stay in Guam to help finish things up if that was OK."

"That's fine. Let's don't interrupt the investigation. If he can just keep us updated," Spencer replied.

Kamaka smiled, said "Thanks, I'll let him know," and quietly pulled the door closed behind him.

Just then the sounds of the Tommy Dorsey Orchestra and Frank Sinatra singing 'Blue Skies' softly enveloped the room. Spencer wasn't sure why the music coming from the old Zenith was so incredibly mellow and soothing, but it was. He wondered if it had been a personal item of Agent Wilson's. He decided that if it wasn't, and it was still there when he retired from that office, he might just have to take it with him.

Spencer continued listening to the Aku morning show for a few more minutes and then returned to the work at hand.

In 1941, the radio station that Spencer was listening to, KGMB, was requested by the military to play continuous music all night to help guide a group of B-17 Flying Fortresses coming from the mainland. The date was Dec. 7. The Japanese used the same continuous music broadcast to help guide them to Pearl Harbor.

As Spencer reviewed each new file, it was obvious that Wilson had kept meticulous records; everything had been done by the book. Nothing seemed to be out of order. Every current assessment and investigation within the department was an example of how things are supposed to be done. He now had a much clearer understanding of the workflow, the agent involvement, and the quality of the man he replaced.

When Spencer turned in his chair to replace the file, he accidently slammed his knee into the corner of the desk.

"Damnit!"

He pulled open the drawer to replace the final file and felt a slight bind in the movement. Thinking nothing of it, he replaced the file, but, as he attempted to close the drawer, it wouldn't push all the way back. It appeared that something had fallen behind the drawer preventing it from closing.

He pulled the drawer out again, leaned over and reached behind the drawer hoping to pull free whatever was blocking it. He could feel nothing, but when he tried, the drawer still wouldn't close completely. He got out of his chair, grabbed the extended drawer by the bottom, and lifted it out of the roller tracks. He carefully sat it on the floor and then looked in the open desk. A file was lying under the drawer wedged against a support bar on the base of the drawer opening.

He pulled out the file, placed it on the desk, and then positioned the drawer back on the roller tracks. The drawer now closed completely. Sitting back in his chair, he focused on the newly discovered file.

Spencer wasn't sure why a file would have been under the drawer. It didn't appear that it could have slipped under by chance. His knee bump must have shifted it to where it obstructed the slide mechanism. For a man who was so well organized and structured in his management style, it made no sense that Wilson would keep a file under the desk drawer.

Again, something else out of place. Spencer's mind immediately began to surmise Wilson's reasoning. It just didn't fit. Unless it was hidden for some reason.

All the files in Wilson's desk drawer had color coded, typed, labels. This file had no label, and it wasn't covered with dust, so it had been accessed recently. Spencer considered locking his office door but realized that might draw attention.

He opened the file.

The top page was a map printed on a single page. The map covered a large portion of the western Pacific Ocean encompassing Hawaii, Guam and Japan. Numerous locations on the map had been underlined. He set the map aside and next picked up a newspaper article cut from the Agana, Guam Dateline. The article discussed beer distribution in the general area of the map. Several sentences in the article had also been underlined.

Spencer then picked up three pages that had been stapled together. The first two pages were filled with notes that were handwritten by, he assumed, Agent Wilson. As he read the notes, he discovered that Wilson was investigating what appeared to be an espionage spy ring in the western pacific working within the area he had of the enclosed map.

Spencer's first thought was why would information of this

importance be hidden in a file kept under the desk drawer in the FBI office in Honolulu. Agent Wilson hadn't done this on a whim. Again, doing things on a whim didn't fit the pattern of a highly structured, by the book agent like Wilson. Spencer realized that this information probably shouldn't be seen by others, so he picked up the file from the top of his desk, pulled out the file drawer and placed the file on top of the others, out of sight.

As he continued reading, it became obvious that the mission of the espionage ring was to provide the Soviet Union with United States Top Secret Cryptographic communications equipment. It listed a Naval Officer, stationed in Japan, as being an embedded spy. Next to that entry was: 'not defined – must be stopped.'

A ripped off portion of a facsimile paper roll was taped below the note on the Naval Spy. It had two printed sets of numbers. They appeared to be a banking account code and routing number. There was nothing else on the strip of paper - just the two sets of numbers.

Below the taped numbers was another hand-written entry that focused on another agent who was coordinating with the naval spy and providing a communication channel between the numerous underlined locations on the map. Next to this entry Wilson had written in red ink: Agana, La Paloma Bar, Agent defined FC 10/12/67. The FC had been overwritten several times as if he were accentuating a point.

The third page of the stapled document had just one ominous handwritten note. Possible informant in office. He had written six letters on the page: C, K, S, V, T, and N. The letters C, K and V had lines drawn threw them as though they had been crossed off the list. Spencer immediately realized that the letters were the first letters of the last names of the agents who had reported to Wilson – and now reported to him. As he studied them, the uncrossed letters S, T, and N seemed to jump off the page.

This explained why Wilson was keeping the investigation close to the vest. There was no indication that he had shared any of what he had learned with anyone in his office. At this point Spencer wasn't going to begin questioning Wilson's judgement. He would keep his mouth shut.

He sat back in his chair and reflected on what he had just read.

His thoughts were well defined. "Jesus Christ, why the hell did I have to stumble into this? Why can't I ever just stick with the easy cases like Sheila said?"

Unfortunately, by nature, Spencer's interest was piqued. It was obvious that any thoughts of quiet days of winding down his career in Hawaii were over.

A knock on his closed door startled him. He placed the stapled sheets he had been reading on his lap before saying, "Come in."

"Sir, we are all headed out, and I wondered if you plan to be here awhile?"

Spencer made a quick glance at his watch. Seeing that it was 1712 hours, he said, "Oh, thanks agent Coleman. I think I'll finish up a few things here before I head out. Got a lot to catch up on," he said smiling. "Is there anything I should know about locking up?"

"You can lock your office door when you leave. We'll lock up out front, so you should just have to close the door behind you. Good night."

"Thank you, Agent Coleman. Have a good evening."

"You do the same." Iris closed the door to Spencer's office as she left.

He waited until he heard them all leave and then moved the file from the file drawer back to the top of the desk.

It was 2030 hours that evening before he had finished the file. The documentation was as thorough and ordered as Mike

Wilson's other investigations. Spencer's respect for this man continued to grow.

He leaned back in his chair and expressed his thoughts. "Jesus Christ!"

A very strong feeling of Deja vu swept over him. The similarity to his last, and unfinished, investigation in Washington DC was surreal. He was, once again, faced with an investigation of international importance that couldn't be discussed with anyone. He stopped to catch his breath.

In the documentation, Mike Wilson had defined a Banner-class environmental research ship, the USS Pueblo. It was scheduled to depart Japan in January 1968 for the waters just outside the international territorial boundaries of North Korea. But the vessel was no longer a research ship. It had been converted to an intelligence gathering vessel that was to monitor North Korea and the Soviet Union. It was a spy ship.

The ship would be fitted with top secret cryptographic communications equipment to send and receive information that had been gathered. Wilson wasn't sure how the Pueblo was of importance.

There was nothing unusual about spy ships being positioned just outside territorial boundaries to monitor activity of other countries. Many countries have their own spy ships doing the very same thing. The question was why this ship, the Pueblo, came to light at all during his investigation.

From the file, it was apparent that Agent Wilson hadn't been able to connect all the dots, but he was close. Spencer guessed that someone else found out just how close he was.

Having read the file, Spencer would have had to have been an idiot to believe the boat explosion that killed Wilson was an accident. It was an obvious act of sabotage. Agent Wilson had to be taken out because he knew too much. And Spencer now had to deal with a possible informant in his own department. An informant who probably was involved in sharing the information that got Wilson killed.

With Wilson out of the picture Spencer surmised that the espionage agents felt that they would be free to proceed with their plan.

Spencer leaned back in his chair and looked up at the fan that was spinning slowly above him. He could pick up a slight hum of the motor as the blades cut through the air. The blades became almost hypnotic as they spun and then came back to the exact position they had started. The analogy to how this case seemed to be headed was not missed by Spencer.

"What the hell is going on here?" he said to himself.

What was important about this spy ship, Pueblo? He continued to watch the fan blades repeating their journey. It was then that the word cryptographic jumped out. He grabbed Wilson's notes again and found the one that read, 'The ship would be fitted with top secret cryptographic communications equipment to send and receive information that had been gathered.'

"Jesus Christ," he almost yelled. "Oh my god!"

A Navy spy ship attached to Naval Intelligence was scheduled to be positioned just off the North Korean coast. The ship would be fitted with Top Secret cryptographic communications equipment. His thoughts jumped to Washington DC and his meeting with Allston Sidwell. An enlisted seaman stationed at Norfolk Virginia had been defined as selling top secret cryptographic code key lists to the Russian Embassy in Washington DC. These two things weren't just happenstance. They had to be connected.

Spencer came back to the realization that he was completely unfamiliar with the wide expanse of ocean and islands that were defined in the file. He was also aware that cryptographic key code lists and communications equipment were something he knew little about. The spy ship was sailing the first of next month to Korea and that didn't leave much time to become educated. His plans of just biding his time quietly until retirement were officially canceled.

Spencer looked at the clock and decided to call it a night. He briefly considered taking the entire file home with him but realized that it was much safer under the drawer in his file cabinet. He opened the file again and found the faxed copy with the bank routing and account number. He wrote down the numbers on a piece of paper and slipped it in his wallet. He closed the file and put it back under the drawer which he then closed and locked. He picked up his briefcase, shut off the lights and locked the door behind him.

The taxi dropped him off at his hotel. Instead of going directly to his room, he walked through the lobby to the restaurant.

"Are you still open for dinner?" he asked the young lady standing near the entrance.

"We are sir. Will it be just you this evening?"

"Yes. And a booth if you have one would be perfect."

"Of course," she replied, "Please follow me."

As he followed the young lady his mind was focused on the file he had found hidden in Wilson's desk. From what little he had learned about Wilson so far, it was obvious that he was a dedicated, meticulous, highly skilled agent. Having read the structured path of facts that Wilson had laid out, Spencer couldn't question the validity of the espionage ring. It was real. And, at the same time, he couldn't question Allston Sidwell's claim from the past week that an enlisted member of the Navy, in Norfolk Virginia was selling Top Secret Cryptographic codes to the Soviets in Washington DC. Sidwell and Wilson had both been murdered because they came too close to the truth. And somehow these two paths to the truth meet. Spencer needed to find out how, and where.

He sat down in the booth, and the young lady handed him a menu, asking, "Sir, can I get you a drink?"

"Oh, yes please. May I have a Dewar's with a splash of water, no ice? Oh, and can you make it a double?"

"A Dewar's, splash of water, no ice, double." she repeated. "I will be right back."

Spencer was fully aware of Sidwell's warning; Wilson's murder; a Russian espionage ring; and an informant in the bureau office in Honolulu. It didn't frighten him, but it did dictate that he move forward extremely carefully.

"And here's your drink Sir," the waitress said as she sat in on the table. "Have you made a selection for dinner, or would you like some more time?"

Spencer pulled away from his thoughts, looked at his watch and then turned to the waitress and said, "You know, I think I'll just have this drink. Didn't realize it was so late. I'm sorry."

"No, no. That's fine," she said with a smile. I'll just bring your check."

Spencer finished his drink and placed the money on the table. He then reached under his jacket and again gripped the handle of his Smith & Wesson. Assured, he slid out of the booth, stood, and walked out of the restaurant. Tomorrow was not going to be a dull day.

CHAPTER 7

Wednesday, November 22, 1967

A light rain was falling as Spencer stepped from the cab in front of the Dillingham Transportation Building. He had had very little sleep. He walked to the elevator and rode to the third floor. As he walked down the hall, he noticed that the smoked glass window emblazoned with the words Federal Bureau of Investigation seemed to be even more ominous that morning.

Upon entering the office, he saw that Coleman and Shuff were on the phone and Kamaka was focused on paperwork. He walked directly to his office without disturbing any of them. Pulling the door closed, he noticed that the office didn't seem to be as stuffy as it had the day before and it was surprisingly cool. He walked to his desk, sat down and unlocked the large file drawer on the bottom right. He slowly pulled it out. Scooting to the front of his chair, he bent over and removed Wilson's hidden file and sat it on top of the very neatly typed, equally spaced and color-coded files that populated the pulled drawer.

One of things that had kept him awake the night before was the small note in Wilson's secret file that said Agana La Paloma Bar,

Agent defined FC 10/12/67.

He had learned on the Monday that he arrived in Hawaii that Agana, Guam, where the field office was located was the capital city of Guam. He had to believe that La Paloma Bar was located in Agana. The FC could be the spy's initials. There might have been some significance about the date, but Spencer had no idea. Perhaps a lot of assumptions, but it was what he had to work with.

A trip to Guam would be understandable for a new Senior Agent coming up to speed on the operations under his command. And in this case, it would provide a perfect cover to follow up on the lead to the spy uncovered by Wilson. The La Paloma would most certainly be one of the stops on the trip.

He stepped to his door and saw Coleman was off her phone.

"Agent Coleman, can I steal you away from your desk for a second? I have a quick question."

"Sure," she replied. "Be right there."

"Agent Coleman," he began." I'd like to schedule a trip to Guam to catch up with Agents Tapper and Neuser and see how things are going with the investigation. It will also give me a chance to get better acquainted with the office over there. Can you tell me how I can get that done?"

"How soon do you want to go?" she asked.

"The investigation is finishing up, so as soon as possible."

"Let me see what I can schedule, Sir."

"Thank you, Agent Coleman."

It was less than twenty minutes later when Coleman knocked on his door.

"Sir, the commercial flights to Guam are booked up for the next week, but we do have an arrangement with the military here where we can sometimes steal a seat on one of their transport planes. When we are sitting in the middle of the Pacific Ocean it just makes sense that we work together. We have helped them out on several situations, and in return, they have helped us when we needed a flight. Anyway, it flies out of Hickam Air Force Base. Just a warning, it's no frills, but it's the fastest way there. They have one scheduled for tomorrow at 3:30."

"Tomorrow afternoon at 3:30?"

"Sorry, no, actually 0330 tonight. Want me to try something else?" she responded.

"No the flight tonight will be fine. Can you check to see if I can get a seat on that flight? That will get me to Guam at about what time?"

"I think it lands at Andersen Air Force Base around noon."

"Perfect. I'll need the afternoon and the next morning to get caught up with Tapper and Neuser," he responded with a smile. "I only plan to be there one night, so if you can possibly get me hooked up for a flight back on the 29th. And I know your job description doesn't include travel agent, but I appreciate the help until I get this figured out."

"Not a problem at all, and I'll check on the return flight."

Just before lunch Agent Coleman again knocked on Spencer's door. He waived her in.

"Sir they do have an open seat on the flight at 330 hours tonight. You are all set; just show up no later than 0245; your paperwork will be at the counter.

"Perfect. Thanks Agent Coleman. Oh, is there any problem carrying my service revolver?"

"None at all. I have already let them know you will be armed."

Iris stood for a moment with her mouth slightly open as if she was going to speak. She then raised both hands as people often do when they are about to share information, and not sure how it's going to be received. It was obvious she was trying to put her next words in a very positive light. "And, sir, coming back you will get to see some of the beautiful islands between here and Guam. You have a seat on the Continental Micronesia Island Hopper."

She stopped for a moment before continuing.

"You might want to take along some reading material because it's about a 16-hour flight with layovers. Sorry, but it was the only thing available."

"Wow, 16 hours. But if I'm stopping on beautiful islands, it will be worth it." he said smiling.

"And again, Agent Coleman I realize travel coordinator is not in your job description. Thank you."

A warm breeze welcomed Spencer as he stepped out of the hotel lobby at 0200 that next morning. A cab pulled up just as he was walking out. The driver rolled down his window and asked, "Did you call for a cab to Hickam?

"I did, wow, you guys are fast."

The ride took about 30 minutes. The cab driver dropped him off at the front gate and drove off. Spencer walked to the armed guard at the gate and said, "I'm agent Spencer with the FBI and I have a seat on a plane that leaves for Guam at 0330."

The Airman asked for some identification. Spencer pulled his FBI badge from his jacket pocket and showed it to him.

"Thank you, sir, and would you also have one other copy of identification. A driver's license perhaps?"

Spencer removed his FBI ID from his wallet and handed it to the guard, who in turn stepped into the guard shack and made a phone call. It was a quick call. The guard stepped back out and handed Spencer his ID.

“Thank you, sir. If you hang on just a second, someone will be here to drive you to the terminal.

A car pulled up to the gate in less than a minute. Spencer thanked the guard and got into the car. It was a quick ride.

The terminal was a makeshift; windowless room built in the corner of a hanger. A small counter was staffed by two airmen. Several neatly placed plastic letters on the board behind them read Guam – 0330.

A dozen chairs that looked like they had been salvaged from a 1940 kitchen set were positioned around the walls. All the vinyl seat covers, and backs were torn. Spencer picked one that looked like it still had a bit of padding. He sat down and looked around the room. Four of the chairs were occupied by uniformed men, presumably waiting for the same flight.

At one point, one of the airmen at the counter mentioned that this was the temporary terminal while the actual terminal was being overhauled. No one in the room seemed interested.

The waiting passengers began boarding at 0310. The five men had their pick of six seats lined against the side of the plane. The rest of the plane was an open bay filled with boxes, equipment, and what appeared to be a casket. No one asked.

They finally landed at Andersen AFB at almost exactly noon, and an Air Police sergeant boarded the plane. He asked that everyone have their orders or paperwork available. Spencer was somewhat surprised that his paperwork caused no concern to the sharply dressed gentleman in perfectly pressed khakis, with a pistol strapped to his hip. A good start, Spencer thought, and kudos to Agent Coleman.

They departed the plane and headed toward the terminal. As they entered, a man stepped forward and asked, “Agent Spencer?”

“Yes, I’m Agent Spencer.”

“Hi, I’m agent Neuser, and this is agent Tapper,” he said gesturing to the man standing next to him. The men both stepped forward to shake Spencer’s hand.

“Well, thank you for picking me up,”

Neuser reached for Spencer’s suitcase, but Spencer said “No, no, thanks, I can grab it.”

The ride from Andersen Air Force Base to Agana led them through little villages named Yigo, and Dededo. Spencer again realized how much of an outsider he must seem. He let the thought drop and asked, “Is there a hotel near the office where I can get a room for tonight?”

“Got you covered,” Neuser replied. When Agent Coleman notified us you were coming I booked you a room in a little hotel just a couple of blocks from the office. It’s small and no frills, but clean and a friendly staff. And there’s a sandwich bar right next door. Again, no frills, but their grinders are pretty good. And you can grab a beer to take back to your room.”

“Perfect. Thanks.”

The car pulled into a small parking lot in front of a two-story concrete block building. The three men walked to the door of the building that displayed a small, somewhat tarnished sign that read Federal Bureau of Investigation. Neuser stopped at the door before they entered and turned, pointing to the right.

“Sir,” if you look just down the street there, you’ll see your hotel. Can’t get much closer than that.”

He unlocked the door and opened it. They all stepped in.

"Not much, but we call it home." Neuser said, followed by a small laugh.

The office was comprised of a room with a desk, a round table with four chairs, and several bookshelves filled with files. A picture of J Edgar Hoover was hanging behind the desk, and a slightly smaller picture of President Johnson hung near the round table. A door to a smaller office was behind the desk to the right. It was obviously Neuser's office.

"We can just set at the table out here, if that's ok sir."

"Of course, perfect," Spencer replied.

Spencer sat his suitcase next to one of the chairs and sat down. The other two men sat across from him.

"Let me begin by saying the same thing I shared with your fellow agents in Honolulu," Spencer began. "It has been a tough couple of weeks for all of you, and now you are faced with working under a Senior Agent who is new to the area. It's going to take all of us some time to get adjusted, but I'm sure we can keep things moving forward. I offer my condolences to both of you for the loss of Agent Wilson. From what I have gathered he was an excellent agent and boss, and a good man. I'm sure he is missed."

The two men both quietly nodded their heads in unison.

"My transfer from the DC office was somewhat rushed and I apologize for any resulting confusion. But we'll work through it."

Neuser replied, "Of course," while Tapper nodded his head slightly.

Spenser reached over and pulled his notepad from his briefcase and set it on the table. He pulled his pen from his shirt pocket and placed it on the pad. As he was adjusting his chair he asked:

"Can we talk about Agent Wilson's accident investigation so I can get up to speed. I understand things are pretty much wrapped up. Where do we stand now?"

Neuser responded first. "We should have the report completed by this afternoon. Because one of the men on the chartered fishing boat was a naval officer, we are working with the Naval Base here in Guam and just waiting for their paperwork. It should be here today.

"Who was the Naval officer?" Spencer interjected.

"A captain Michael Wise. We know he was one of the regulars on the fishing trips. He worked at the base here in Guam, and according to the information we have, he worked in the Legal department. He obviously knew Agent Wilson, but not sure if they were close friends."

"OK, Thanks." Spencer made a note on his notepad.

"And because the officer and an FBI Senior Agent died in the accident, we naturally reviewed any possible threat of sabotage. But from everything we have uncovered so far, this was just a terrible accident."

Neuser pulled a sheet of paper from his file and handed it to Spencer. "Here is a list of the names of the men on the boat, along with a brief overview of their backgrounds."

"I understand there was one survivor?" Spencer enquired.

Neuser replied, "There was one survivor, a Tim Curry. He is a distributor for Heineken beer and the host of the fishing trip. He held these fishing trips several times a year. Although I believe this one was kind of a special one that was put together fairly quickly. Tim said it was the company financial year end, and he was trying to use up as much of his fun money as he could before it ran out.

"Do you know Mr. Curry personally?" Spencer asked.

"I do. I met him the first week I transferred here a couple of years ago. He's a good guy. Agent Wilson had known him even longer than I had. They became friends and because they both enjoyed fishing, Agent Wilson always seemed to be invited to these outings. He tried to schedule his bi-annual business visits to Guam to coincide with the trips. He couldn't make them all, of course, but this one he did, unfortunately."

"Where is Mr. Curry now?"

"He just got back from the states. He had flown back to see his folks for a few days to just get away from everything. I think he got back on Monday and is already back to work."

"He recovered faster than I would have after something like that." Spencer commented.

"Can't imagine." Neuser added.

The men continued discussing the 'accident' for the next half hour, while Spencer took notes.

There was nothing that came up in the discussion that swayed Spencer's belief that the boat explosion was not an accident, but either one of these men could be the informant Wilson had suspected, and Spencer couldn't show his hand.

To this end he added, "And these poor guys were just out for a fishing trip. What a horrible waste of life. Just a terrible accident."

Neuser responded with, "This is just not fair."

"Life isn't fair John," Tapper added, "But this is total crap."

The three men sat quietly for several seconds reflecting on the situation.

Spencer broke the silence by adding, "I know you have both been working on this for some time and have got things pretty much wrapped up, but if there is anything at all I can do to help with the investigation please let me know."

"Thank you, Sir," Neuser replied

Spencer then turned to Tapper. "Agent, I know you've got to get to the airport, and I understand you were lucky enough to get a seat on a commercial flight back to Hawaii. They were booked up by the time my flight was scheduled, so I will be headed back tomorrow on the Continental Micronesia Island Hopper. I've been told I'm taking the scenic route."

The three men laughed, and Neuser added, "Hey, you haven't been initiated to the islands until you've flown the Hopper."

"Well, have a safe trip, Agent. We'll get together when I get back." Spence added.

Neuser took a couple of steps toward Tapper, smiled, and held out his hand. "Bill, thanks for your help. Have a safe trip back and we'll catch up later. I think it's my turn to buy drinks next time."

Tapper headed to the airport and Spencer and Neuser spent twenty minutes going over his current investigations. It was just after 0330 hours when they finished.

"John, I think I'm going to head to the hotel and crash for the night, I'll stop back in tomorrow morning before I catch my flight back. Thanks for bringing me up to date."

"Sure thing, Sir. Not sure how you lasted as long as you have. I'm guessing you didn't get any sleep last night."

"It has been a long day," Spencer replied.

They shook hands and he picked up his suitcase and walked to the hotel. The lady at the front desk, by the name of Naomi, he was to learn, was very friendly as she gave him his room key and said she hoped he enjoyed his stay. He thanked her and then walked back outside and down to his room to change into something more casual. His focus now was on The La Paloma Bar.

He stopped again at the hotel lobby and asked Naomi how he might get a cab. She immediately called a number she had obviously memorized, and a cab arrived in short order.

The La Paloma Bar was a single-story pole building separated from the beach only by a narrow, partially sand covered, two lane road. The two sides of the building with the ocean view had screens running from the three-foot-high windowsills to the top of the windows. The remaining two sides had plywood running from floor to ceiling. The weathered walls had hints of about five different colors of peeling paint. Shutters that opened from the outside on the windows with the ocean view were pushed back and haphazardly tied with twine providing a panoramic view of the Philippine Sea.

Spencer opened the screen door and walked in. The door slammed behind him. A long bar occupied the space toward the back and about 10 tables were scattered around the open area. Two of the tables had been pushed together and a group of 6 men were enjoying their beer and talking. A couple of men sat at the far end of the bar, but plenty of stools were open so he walked to the bar and sat down.

The bartender, who was chatting with the two guys at the bar, yelled over; "What can I get you?"

"Can I have a Dewars'?"

"Sorry, out of Dewars'. Got Johnny Walker and J&B?"

"Hey, Johnny Walker would be fine," Spencer responded.

"Good. Not restocked yet with Dewar's. Supposed to have a shipment coming in tomorrow, but I'm guessing you'd rather not wait."

"I can tell you've been doing this awhile." Spencer said, laughing.

"Oh, just a splash of water, no ice. And make it a double."

"You got it."

Spencer picked up his drink and looked around the room. A metal roof doubled as a painted ceiling, and four, large, suspended fans, hanging from weathered rafters, were spinning slowly. His mind was focused on the scribbled note that he found in Wilson's file.

La Paloma Bar, Agent defined FC 10/12/67.

There was a lot that could be read into the note, but Spencer's gut told him that Wilson wasn't the only one who knew he had defined the agent, and it was probably what got him killed. He also had a feeling that FC was a frequent guest of La Paloma.

Spencer finished his drink and called the bartender. "Can I get one more of these?"

"Sure thing," the bartender replied. "Johnny Walker, splash of water, no ice, double, right?"

"That's it."

Just as the bartender delivered the drink, the screen door slammed, and the bartender turned toward the door and yelled "Hey Timmy! Let me guess, you could use a cold beer."

Spencer turned to see a slim, well-conditioned man of about six feet, probably in his late thirties entering. He was wearing a white, short-sleeved polo shirt with a Heineken logo.

He headed to the far end of the bar and sat next to the two guys who were talking with the bartender. As he sat down, the bartender slid a cold Heineken in front of him.

"You guys new here?" Timmy asked the two men.

"Yeah, we're crew members on a freighter that's headed out in the morning. Thought we'd grab a beer or two before we head back."

"Well, that being the case let me buy you one."

"Sure, I'll have a Bud." One of the men said.

"Budweiser! Well, then you'll have to buy your own." He then smiled and said, "If you say Heineken then the drinks are on me." Both guys said Heineken was perfect.

"Why you pushin Heineken?" the other guy asked.

The bartender jumped in and said, "Timmy here is the Heineken distributor for the Western Pacific. Here every Thursday afternoon. He travels from Japan to Hawaii to Guam and every island in-between and spends his work hours in bars buying drinks. Who the hells lucky enough to get a job like that!?" the bartender laughed with a roar.

Spencer had a flash back of the picture he saw in Wilson's office and the discussion he had just had with Neuser and Tapper. Surely, he couldn't have been so lucky to drop into a bar in Guam on a Thursday afternoon and run into the only survivor of the fishing boat explosion.

Spencer finished his drink, thanked the bartender, and left some cash on the bar.

Before he got up to leave, he asked if there was any way to catch a cab.

"Got you covered," the bartender replied as he picked up the phone.

He hung up and said, "Billy will be here in about 5 minutes. Best cab driver in the area. Well, actually the only cab driver in the area." The bartender laughed and gave Spencer a thumbs up.

Now was not the time to start a conversation with Timmy about the tragic 'accident.' However, he did now have a face for the headless guy in the photo. But if the explosion wasn't an accident, this Timmy had to be involved somehow. Spencer wondered if Wilson had missed this.

Whatever the case, Wilson had defined someone with the initials FC. Spencer realized his chances of finding this FC were slim at best. And he couldn't raise anyone's suspicions by asking questions.

Spencer walked outside, avoiding slamming the screen door as he exited, and waited for Billy. An old Toyota with a faded sign on the door that read, Billy's Cab pulled up in less than five minutes. Billy, Spencer found out, was a talker and Spencer was exhausted – small talk was difficult. He was glad when Billy pulled up in front of the hotel.

Spencer stopped in the sandwich bar next to the hotel and bought a sandwich and a couple of cold beers. He spent that evening sitting on the bed in his hotel room, eating the sandwich, drinking the beers, and thinking. He needed to scribble down some thoughts, but his brief case was across the room, out of reach, and just the idea of getting out of bed and walking five feet seemed like a stretch. He realized he hadn't slept for two nights.

He leaned over and pulled open the drawer in the bed stand next to him hoping there might be a writing pad and a pen. He was in luck; there were a couple of pencils, a small pad of paper and a 1967 calendar. He took the note pad and a pencil, sat it on the top of the bed stand and reached for the calendar. His eyes were immediately drawn to October 12 – it was a Thursday. Pieces were beginning to fall into place. FC 10/12/67. Wilson defined the agent at Wally's on a Thursday – the same day Tim Curry, made his weekly stop. His thoughts were becoming more focused.

Spencer finished his sandwich and the two beers. He then removed his clothes and hung them in the closet. After a quick shower, he walked back to the bed and fell asleep almost immediately.

The next morning Spencer checked out and walked to the Bureau office with his suitcase and briefcase. A warm breeze was blowing, and the palm trees swayed gently. He thought about the cold rain that greeted him to work in the DC office just a few weeks earlier. There were some obvious benefits to working in the islands.

Spencer opened the door of the concrete block building and walked in. Neuser yelled from his office, "Come in and grab a seat. I'll be off this call in a minute."

Spencer sat has suitcase on the floor and placed his briefcase on the table and opened it. He pulled out the notes he had taken during the meeting with Neuser and Tapper the day before and began to review them. There was really nothing in the notes that he was interested in, but he wanted this trip and this meeting to look like nothing unusual. There would be no mention of his stop in The La Paloma Bar the night before or his chance sighting of the Heineken distributor. Too close to home.

Neuser finished his call and walked into the front office.

"How was your evening?" he asked Spencer.

"Good. The hotel was fine, and I did pick up a meatball grinder and a couple of beers to take back to the room. Not sure if it was because I was starved, but the sandwich was delicious," he said with a smile.

"I'm headed back at 1:00 so we have plenty of time if you have any questions. I have gone over the notes, and it looks like you've got everything under control."

Spencer looked down at his pad and then said, "Oh, there is one thing. I must have missed the notes on how Curry managed to escape the explosion. Can you check that for me?"

"Oh, it should be in there," Neuser responded. "Let me check the report again, just so we get everything."

He walked into his office to grab the page in question. While he was looking, he yelled from the office, "The boat was a brand-new Hatteras 50' Yacht Fisherman.
It had twin, inboard, Diesel engines. Diesel has a high flash point, so we assume the explosion was caused by a propane tank they had on board for the stove and heater. The tank must have been leaking for an explosion like that, but if that were the case, there was no indication what caused the leak."

He walked back into the front office and sat down across from Spencer. As he was reviewing the page, he continued, "Here it is. It's pretty much cut and dry. Curry stated that it had begun raining quite heavily, so the group moved below into the cabin for some beer and food. He said that he had just stepped out of the cabin and was at the stern of the boat grabbing some more beers out of the coolers. Apparently, they had worked through all the ones they had in the cabin. The last thing he remembers was a huge explosion and he found himself floating in the ocean. The boat was completely engulfed in flames, and he remembered pieces of fiberglass and wood falling around him. He saw a large piece of the cabin wall floating nearby and he somehow managed to pull himself on to it. From that point he only remembers fading in and out of consciousness until he woke up lying on the floor of a fishing boat with three guys staring down at him. He discovered that they had seen the explosion from a distance and came to his rescue."

"And no other men found?" Spencer asked.

"No," Neuser replied, "the water depth in that part of the ocean is about 32,000 ft. All these islands are at the edge of the Marianas Trench, the deepest part of the ocean in the world. And it was in an area that is known for sharks. Probably no chance any of them will ever be found."

Spencer was impressed with the convenience of the story that Curry had related.

"So, Curry was floating on a piece of the boat in the deepest ocean in the world with sharks around before he was discovered. Jesus, one lucky guy!"

"When he got to the medical clinic on Rota," Neuser replied, "the doctor said he probably used up eight of his nine lives. He told me all the doctor could say was, "Francis Curry, you are one lucky son of a bitch. They kept him overnight for observation, but he was fine. Some burns on his one arm, but that was it. He was released the next morning.

"Wait a minute, Francis? I thought I wrote down that his name was Timmy."

"Oh, his first name is Francis, but he hates it, so he goes by his middle name, Timothy. Everybody always calls him Timmy. The only person I ever remember calling him Francis was Agent Wilson, but I suspect he did that just because he knew Timmy hated it, and they were always needling each other." Neuser said, smiling.

"Thanks," Spencer replied. "Francis Curry. Got it."

FC 10/12/67

CHAPTER 8

Saturday, November 25

The flight back from Guam took a little more than 16 hours. Spencer looked at his watch as the plane landed. It was 1715. The Continental Micronesia Island Hopper had stopped at five islands on its way back to Hawaii. He had now begun to appreciate the vastness of his Pacific back yard. Unfortunately, he only managed to get a couple of hours sleep on the flight. It was Saturday morning, but he was hoping he could get into the office to pick up Wilson's file to take back to the hotel for the weekend.

The cab driver dropped Spencer off at his hotel, where he quickly showered, changed clothes and headed back to Bishop Street. Agent Coleman had given him a front hall door key, so he should have no problem getting in. He just hoped to hell no one was in the office.

The office was empty. He picked up the file, locked up, and again went back to his hotel. It was going to be a long weekend reviewing – again - every shred of paper Wilson had hidden.

His first full weekend in Hawaii, and it was spent tied up in a hotel, living off takeaway from the restaurant next door. But for

Spencer it was time well spent. He was now up to speed with Wilson – well, to just before he was murdered.

Monday Morning November 27

"Good morning, Sir," agent Coleman said as he walked in the door. "How was the trip?"

"Good morning. It was a good trip, and I now know what the Guam office looks like," he said with a smile. "And thanks again for setting up the flights and coordinating everything with the office on Guam."

Agent Coleman smiled and said, "You are very welcome."

"I promise next time I take a trip I won't stick you with making all of the arrangements Iris." He then smiled and leaned in toward Coleman and whispered, "I'll ask Agent Shuff."

They were both laughing, quietly as he turned to walk to his office.
Kamaka was on the phone but gave a brief wave as he walked by. Shuff made no effort to acknowledge his arrival. Agent Tapper said, "Good Morning, Sir. Looks like you survived the Hopper. Welcome back."

Spencer laughed and responded, "Thanks, I did survive. It was an experience."

"Trust me, I know." Tapper responded, laughing.

"Oh, Agent Tapper," Spencer continued, "let's get together after lunch to go over your investigations if you are available." Tapper nodded and replied, "Sure thing, Sir, just let me know."

Spencer unlocked his office door, walked in and closed the door behind him. The room was a bit warm, so he opened the window, turned on the fan and sat down. He pulled out the desk drawer and removed the framed picture. The headless man with the Heineken shirt had now been identified.

The final report on the boating accident should arrive the next day, but Spencer had no expectations that anything other than an 'accident' would be officially noted.

He would also have to assume that if his office had been searched by the people who were trying to silence Wilson, they did not find the hidden file - the file that only Spencer now knew existed. Iris said that his office hadn't been entered since Wilson had left for the chartered fishing trip, but if it had been searched and Iris wasn't aware that it had, it would have been done when the office was closed. He was again acutely aware of the significance of what he had stumbled on. He was also aware that there was no one in the office who could be trusted.

As the replacement for Wilson, Spencer knew that if there was a saboteur in the office, he, or she, would be watching him carefully. If it appeared that he was not aware of the espionage ring that Wilson had uncovered, it would be to their benefit that he remained in his position. After all, he was only in Honolulu to ride out his last few years before retirement. The assumption would be that he was not about to pick up any investigation that wasn't already on the books or didn't evolve through the daily work of the agents in the office. Spencer, they would assume, would be retired within a few years, and with Wilson gone, their tracks were covered.

Although there were the few things that were missing in Wilson's investigation, he had systematically defined an expansive operation that had been orchestrated by the navy spy and the Russians. The depth and control of the operation was frightening. And it appeared that the only thing that stood between their success and being stopped was him. But, again, he was flying without a net, and he knew it.

It was time to involve Sheila. He needed help.

He glanced at his watch as he considered the time difference in Washington. He realized it would be the middle of the night for Sheila, but he needed to catch her before she left for work in the morning and calling her at her office was not an option. A phone call from him in the middle of the night wouldn't be unusual, but this would be one that she wouldn't expect.

He picked up his jacket and headed out. "Agent Coleman, I'm running out for a minute. Be right back," he said as he walked to the hall door in the main office area. Spencer walked out of the building and turned toward his hotel. He had noticed a payphone just around the corner by the drugstore. He would be out of sight there and could talk freely.

When he got to the phone, he picked up the handset and put a dime in the slot. The phone came to life with a dial tone. He dialed the long-distance operator, put in the required money and then waited.

"After about a minute, he heard a somewhat sleepy, "Hello."

"Hi Sheila, this is James."

"What? James. Are you OK? What time is it?"

"I'm fine, and I know it's about 0130 there. I'm sorry I woke you, but I need to talk."

"No, no, it's fine. What's going on?"

"I've found myself in another one of those hard cases you told me to avoid."

"What are you talking about, James?"

"This might even be bigger than the Norfolk spy. I really need your help, Sheila."

"I'm almost afraid to ask what you got yourself into this time, James, but of course, you can count me in."

He kept the conversation as brief as he possibly could. He told her about the hidden investigation file that Wilson was keeping and the spy ship that was scheduled to leave Japan to be stationed just off North Korea. He shared that he was sure the stolen top secret crypto key code lists from the naval base in Virginia and the spy ship filled with crypto equipment and documentation were related.

By now, Sheila was completely awake and following every word. She agreed completely with James about his observation. "There is no way this is a just coincidence. But James do you really want to jump into this? I thought you were just riding out your time."

"Guess riding out my time wasn't in the cards."

"What do you need James. Things are getting kind of boring here anyway."

"I could use a couple of things. First, I need to talk with one of your contacts over here who has a good understanding of the interworking of the Navy in the South Pacific. If I try to get anywhere near this there will be red flags going up and we need to avoid that at any cost. I need some strategic background, and I don't have the means of gathering it quickly. I need to talk to one of your top informants."

"I understand," Sheila replied.

"I don't want you putting yourself in danger with this Sheila. This is probably just a crazy idea that won't come to fruition, so losing your job, or worse, is not an option. If it starts to look iffy, back out immediately."

"Understand. What's your next thing, James?"

"Wilson had a fax copy with two strings of numbers. They look like bank account and routing numbers. The numbers were taped into his file next to the information on the spy that is embedded with the Navy in Japan. I don't know what they have to do with all of this, but is there some way you can trace them?"

"Hey, it will be a cakewalk."

Spencer read the numbers to Sheila who wrote them down. She read back the numbers to James to make sure she had them correct.

"James, it looks like it might be an account in the UOB in Hong Kong, but I'll confirm that. Are you looking for anything other than the owner?"

"I'm hoping we can get a name, the amount in the account and how the money got there. If Wilson was on the right track with this, and my guess is he was, we should be able to trace it back to the spy. Then we'll have enough to..." He stopped for a second. "I was going to say take this to the U.S. Attorney for prosecution, but we can't take this to anybody. Christ! The only option we have is to find the bastard and try to stop the Pueblo from sailing.

"OK James, I got it. I'll get back to you when I have the information."

"How are you concealing this investigation?" she asked.

"Actually, Carson told me to take a week off to do some apartment hunting and get settled in once I got here. So, I will be officially on vacation, and my absence from the office won't be questioned."

"I'll get this information back to you as soon as I can James."

"How are things getting sorted back in Washington?" He asked. "Are you picking up any noise on the Hampton situation.?"

"It's been quiet. I haven't heard a thing."

"Good. And Sheila, I promise this isn't going to disrupt our plans. I will be finding us an apartment while I am taking the time off. I hate not having you here with me in Hawaii, so please be careful.

I love you."

"I will, James. I love you too."

He hung up the phone and could only wait.

CHAPTER 9

FBI Building, Washington DC

Tuesday November 28, 1967

Sheila's day began with a phone call to Yi-Chun Li in Taipei, Republic of China. Li was her top intelligence contact for the Pacific. A call to Taiwan would be nothing out of the ordinary for Sheila, and it wouldn't pique anyone's interest at the bureau. The call lasted a little over 10 minutes. It wasn't unusual to have to re-dial several times for an overseas call of that duration, but the circuits held that morning and only the one call was required. Sheila hoped it was a good sign.

Her secret discussion with Li concluded with an arranged meeting in Taipei with James. She then moved on to coordinating flights and money transfers for James to make the meeting possible. It was several hours past her normal quitting time before she had things arranged, but there was still one final job to finish that evening.

She glanced at her watch. It was just past 1930 hours. The sun had been down for several hours and most of the offices in her section of the WFO were dark. Other than the sound of an occasional door closing and the hushed echo of voices saying goodnight, the empty hallway outside her office was quiet.

Sheila's one final task that evening was to send a teletype message to Hong Kong at exactly 2000 hours. Her normal procedure for a teletype or facsimile transmission was to either send the request through interoffice mail or drop it off in the communication center.

Tonight, was different. Tonight no one could know about the transmission. She had gone over in her head a dozen times the warnings of caution from Spencer and the possible ramifications of someone learning of her involvement with him. Her job would certainly be in jeopardy if she were to be found out. And, if she were to be discovered working with James, she could easily be targeted by the same people who had had Sidwell killed. Sheila understood the real danger she would be in if she were to be discovered with the message - but the message was still going to be transmitted at exactly 2000 hours that evening.

The account number that Spencer had given her was associated with the bank in Hong Kong as she had suspected. She, fortunately, was quite familiar with the bank and had worked with them on numerous occasions over the years; mostly concerning money laundering and illegal wire transfers and wire fraud. Her direct contact at the bank, a Mr. Thomas Chen, Vice President of International Finances, had become a valuable and highly trusted friend. They had established and nurtured a very successful and mutually beneficial working relationship beginning with their first introduction in Hong Kong.

Thomas was a somewhat flamboyant, highly educated, extremely well-dressed, refined gentleman of about forty. He had grown accustomed to the finest tailors, the finest restaurants, the finest cars and, of course, the finest apartments in an extremely expensive city. He had been born into a wealthy family in China who, as a result of his father's work, found themselves transferred to Hong Kong when he was six years old.

It was apparent to anyone who met Thomas, even at that young age, that he was a gifted child. His years in primary, junior and senior secondary education, were challenging only by his desire to learn more.

Having completed his undergraduate studies at University of Hong Kong he moved to the United States to complete his education at first Columbia and then the University of Pennsylvania. He presented his doctoral viva on international finance to the faculty dissertation committee when he was twenty-two. His oral defense was flawless.

That evening Thomas's discreet personal involvement in the soon to be transmitted request was crucial. The information could go no further than him.

A message from Sheila the day before had notified him to expect the private transmission the next morning. Chen acknowledged her message and assured her he would be standing by the teletype to retrieve it.

At eight o'clock in the morning, the message would begin printing on the receiving teletype at the bank. The day would just be starting in Hong Kong, and if he wasn't there before the message printed, another employee could easily pick it up. That could not happen. Chen had to be the only employee at the bank to see this teletype message.

Sheila glanced at her watch again for about the fifth time. She knew – or at least prayed - that the communications center at the WFO would be empty at this hour of night. She hoped no one would acknowledge her while she was in the room.

At exactly 1945 she walked out of her office and down the hall to the comm center. In the pocket of her jacket was a folded piece of paper, containing the account number, and routing numbers for her contact in Hong Kong.

The clanking sound of her high heels on the tile floor seemed amplified as it reverberated throughout the empty corridors of the building. When she reached the room, she glanced in the door window and was relieved to find that the room was empty other than the two evening shift employees who were busy typing. Sheila opened the door quietly, walked in, and without acknowledging the two women - who fortunately were deeply focused on their work - sat in a chair in front of a Model 33 ASR Teletype. The position of the machine allowed her to observe anyone walking by or coming into the room.

Sheila was very familiar with the Model 33 Teletype. At one time, she was the new employee who had been tasked with sending and receiving department teletype messages when they were deemed too urgent to wait in the 'to do' pile until the communication center finally got around to sending them. It seemed to Sheila that every request back then was deemed too urgent to wait, and as a result, she became quite proficient in using the machine.

She took a slow, deep breath as she gave the teletype a quick once-over. She then checked to see if the paper punch tape was in place and the paper roll was loaded. Out of habit, she unclipped the plastic tape feeder holder, rechecked the punch tape positioning, and then clipped it back in place securely. Having to retype a message because the paper tape jammed was something you learned to avoid early on.

She then pulled the paper from her jacket pocket, unfolded it and placed it in the document holder over the keyboard. She began typing; first the subscriber code followed by THOM and then the country code for Hong Kong. The message would be routed to the teletype in the bank in Hong Kong. The message was short: Thomas Chen. Urgent. Secret. Need all available info on following account. Please advise when ready. SA. She then typed in the account code and routing number that Spencer had found in Wilson's hidden file.

She advanced the paper roll and tore off the printed message. She compared it to her handwritten note to make sure she hadn't made any typing errors. The message was correct. She folded the ripped off piece of paper from the teletype and put in her pocket.

She checked her watch – 1955. She carefully tore off the now punched tape and positioned it in the tape reader. With one hand on the start lever, ready to begin the transmission at exactly 2000 hours, her eyes remained focused on her watch. 1956 hours. She could feel her heart beating in her chest. The second hand on her watch seemed to be running slower.

"Anderson! What are you doing at a teletype? Don't you have people for that?"

The voice startled her. She looked up to see Mark Williams walking toward her.

"Shit!" Her silent expletive reflected her concern that he might have seen how he had startled her, and her concern that he found her at the teletype at almost eight o'clock at night.

Without removing her eyes from Williams, she quickly removed the piece of paper from the document holder and placed it on her lap. She then deftly unclipped the tape holder, pulled the punched tape from the machine, rolled the tape and hid it in the palm of her left hand.

While doing this she responded to the one person she despised at the WFO, "Agent Williams, how are you doing this evening? And to answer your question, this request came in after our department secretary had left for the evening. So here I am."

He walked toward Sheila and stopped directly in front of the teletype she was setting at. She carefully slid the folded paper further down her lap. He leaned forward and looked over the top of the teletype.

"What secret message are you getting in tonight, Anderson; or are you sending out?"

She thanked God that she had ripped off the typed message.

"You must be waiting for something, because there's no tape in the reader. I'm not as familiar with these machines as you are, obviously, but don't you usually use a punched tape to send a message?"

She gripped the punched tape in her hand.

Hoping that her voice wasn't quavering, she responded, "Williams, don't you have something else you should be doing besides running around checking up on other people? I would think your time could be better spent."

"Hey, Anderson, I came in for a facsimile and thought I would be polite and say hello. But it looks like you're concerned somebody's going to discover you're doing something you shouldn't be doing, so I'll just leave you at it. Have a nice evening." He laughed under his breath as he walked away.

She responded with, "Asshole!" but, unfortunately, she suspected that he didn't hear her.

Williams stopped at the door and turned back to Sheila. "Hey Anderson, what ever happened to your old compadre Spencer? You guys were pretty close, weren't you? I heard he got booted out for some reason. You hear anything?"

Sheila responded without missing a beat. "I'm the last one who hears anything around here. I don't have a clue."

"Just wondered," he replied as he turned and walked out the door.

Her watch read 1959.

"Jesus!"

She unrolled the punched tape, placed it back in the tape reader and pressed the run lever just as the second hand on her watch signaled 2000 hours.

The reader pulled the tape in and quickly read the punched message. The paper tape fell into a small bin positioned under the reader. Sheila retrieved the tape. She then waited for an identifying code verifying that the message had been routed to the correct recipient. She couldn't leave until she had received the code. As she waited, she moved the folded letter from her lap to her coat pocket.

Knowing Williams, he would be walking back in the room and pressing her for more information. Her breath was rapid; her heart was still pounding. The teletype finally came to life and printed the verifying code. The message had been routed correctly. She advanced the paper, ripped off the returned code, put it and the punched tape in her pocket and walked to the door. She opened the door and glanced both ways down the hall. The hall was empty. She walked back to her office.

Her heart had stopped pounding and the sound of her heels in the hallway didn't seem quite as loud.

The Next Morning

Sheila arrived at work the next morning anticipating a normal workday. The teletype message to Chen had been received by him less than twelve hours earlier and she didn't expect hearing from him until at least the next day. And, if Williams happened to pursue his questions about finding her in the communications center the night before, she knew it would be easy to explain them away and direct him to find some other agent's questionable actions to focus on.

She had just walked into her office, hung her coat on the rack and, was removing her scarf when the phone rang.

"Hello, this is Anderson."

"You have an overseas call coming in, Agent Anderson, should I patch it through?"

"Yes, please."

After several clicks and some static; "Hello, Agent Anderson?"

She recognized the voice immediately. "Thomas, this is Sheila."

"Your volume is a bit weak, but I can hear you. Can you hear me?" he asked.

"Yes, I can hear you, Thomas."

Guessing that he couldn't have pulled together all the information on the bank account so quickly, she asked, "Was there a problem with the transmission I sent?"

"No. To the contrary, it came through perfectly. I have already gathered the information you requested. I was going to arrange a teletype transmission, but the information appears to be too sensitive to chance being viewed by anyone else. I have sent the information in an envelope by First Class currier directly to you. It will be going out the next flight to DC, and it will arrive at your office tomorrow morning."

"Thank you, Thomas! That is perfect."

"It was no problem, of course." Chen replied. "I will say Sheila that what you have uncovered should be addressed immediately. Your request has opened the window to a very sinister situation. Please be careful as you move forward with this. Let me know if I can be of further assistance. We will talk soon."

Sheila quickly sat the handset back on the switch hook of the phone. She then finished removing her scarf from around her neck, hung it on the rack, and walked to the break room where she poured herself a cup of coffee. She would have to wait until the next day for Chen's envelope, so she returned to her office to focus on outstanding projects. Fortunately, the time seemed to fly by.

At exactly 1700 she draped her scarf around her neck, put on her coat and headed to her car. She was thankful that she had managed to remain busy all day. She was also thankful that her wine rack at home was fully stocked.

CHAPTER 10

Sheila arrived at work early on that Wednesday. She had spent a restless night wondering about the report from Thomas Chen that was expected that morning. She kept herself busy while waiting for the mail delivery. It usually arrived at 0830, but it was almost 1000 hours before it finally reached her desk. She waited anxiously while the mail delivery cart stopped outside the door of her office and a young man sorted through the stacks of mail and packages.

"Good morning, Agent Anderson," he said as he opened the door and stepped in. "Sorry I'm a little late this morning, but Jenny called in sick today, and we got behind in the mail room."

"Good morning, John," Sheila replied, smiling. "Not a problem. Hope Jenny is feeling better soon."

"Somebody said they thought it was the flu, but she said she'd be in tomorrow, so I'm guessing it's not that." He handed Sheila her mail.

"Thanks, John. Have a great day."

"Thanks, you too," he replied smiling. He closed the door behind him; spent a minute sorting the mail again and then pushed his cart to the next office.

She quickly perused the envelopes and pulled one from the pile. A stamp on the envelope showed that it had been sent by international courier. The return address on the envelope was Hong Kong.

"Thank God!" she said to herself.

Amazed that Thomas had been able to pull together the information on the account so quickly, she hoped that it was thorough enough to specifically answer the questions relating to the Navy spy in Japan. She needed names, affiliations and a solid link of money trails for any funds in the account. Sheila opened the envelope and removed four neatly folded pages.

Thomas and Sheila had worked together for over five years, and during that time, had been able to stop the flow of hundreds of millions of dollars in laundered money and illegally acquired funds. Their efforts subsequently led to the arrest and conviction of thugs ranging from international drug dealers, gangs, and the mafia to high-ranking elected officials in countries worldwide.

A fair portion of the confiscated money from each conviction was ultimately returned to the bank as a payment for their assistance. Thomas Chen, as a result, became a highly valued member of the banking team. He was given the freedom to work with international investigative organizations, like the FBI, who could provide unequivocal evidence that the information that was being requested was the result of investigations showing that international laws were being broken. He used the freedom wisely. Sheila appreciated the position of the bank and had always approached them through proper legal channels.

The request for information on this matter, however, was quite a bit different, and the dispersion of any funds that might become available would not go to the bank, but to Thomas Chen directly. The bank would remain completely unaware of this transaction.

If the detailed observations in Agent Wilson's hidden file were correct, an embedded spy at the naval base in Japan was planning to facilitate the delivery of United States Top Secret Electronic coding equipment to the Soviet Union. To prevent this from happening, time was of the utmost importance - but time was something they had little of.

Thomas Chen had a unique way of filtering through the boilerplate and filler in elaborate financial transactions and banking documentation. His mind worked like Sheila's. Just give me the facts; I don't have time for all the crap surrounding it.

Sheila began reading. The first page began simply. Single account holder: William Andrew Mason. Current account total: $16,457,014.23 US.

She read the account holder and total again. "What? Jesus Christ!"

She continued reading, and found that Chen had provided documented proof of multiple money trails from five foreign governments to shell companies in Hong Kong, Singapore, Panama, Bahamas, and the Isle of Man. In turn, each of these 'companies' was funneling the funds to a dummy corporation named Assets Unlimited that was based on paper, in Hong Kong. It further showed that all monies for Assets Unlimited were being wired to the bank account James had given to her.

Sheila had learned early on that the adage, 'follow the money' was always the right path. And in this case, all the money could be followed directly to the account of a William Andrew Mason. If all of this panned out, the naval officer Agent Wilson had uncovered as an embedded spy in Japan now had a name.

The documentation also showed that the five foreign government entities were structuring payment through each of the five shell companies. The deposits were being split into five equal payments, with one fifth wired to each company. It was a common practice in money laundering so that it would be harder to trace. To the bank the transitions appeared legitimate, and with Hong Kong being a tax haven, there were no red flags raised over tax regulations. All the financial transactions had gone unnoticed for years. The person who was coordinating all of this obviously had an exceptional grasp of international fund transfers, and was acutely aware of the need, and methods to hide the funding activity.

With the amount of money that was documented in Mason's account in Hong Kong, the logical explanation would be that he had, in fact, been profiting in espionage by selling extremely sensitive secret United States military information to the foreign countries who were willing to pay huge amounts of money to obtain. It was safe to assume he hadn't amassed his fortune selling tickets to the annual Army/Navy football game.

She sat at her desk for a few minutes reviewing what she had just read. She then reached for her rolodex, flipped through several cards and then picked up her phone and called a number at the Department of the Navy. A final confirmation that this, in fact, was the navy spy.

Obviously, the Navy would become suspicious if questions were raised by the FBI about one of their officers, but Sheila had several confidential contacts at lower levels of the department who owed her for information she had provided over the years. Today, she would call in some of those chips.

"Captain Taylor, this is Sheila Anderson at the FBI. Do you have a couple of seconds?"

"Yes, of course." He replied.

She told him that she had several questions concerning a confidential matter.

He listened to her questions and then promised to get back to her within the hour.

Sheila sat back in her chair and carefully read the four pages again. She then placed the folded pages back in the envelope and put the envelope in her purse...and waited.

It was forty-five minutes from the time she called Captain Taylor when her phone rang. She picked it up and identified herself.

"Miss Anderson, you didn't hear any of this from me, but ...."

Captain Taylor shared that a Captain William Andrew Mason was a highly decorated naval officer currently stationed at the base in Yokosuka, Japan. He was scheduled to be discharged from the Navy in six months. In answer to her second question, Captain Mason held a master's degree in international finance.

She thanked Captain Taylor for his quick response and assured him that she hadn't heard any of this from him.

Sheila needed to get a telegram to James ASAP. But first she needed to have the sixteen and a half million dollars moved from the account of William Mason into another account that would be better suited to hold the funds. Moving the funds to a non-traceable account would put an immediate and very sizable financial dent in the highly decorated Naval Officer's future. She just wished she could be there to see the look on his face when he next checked his holdings account. She couldn't help but smile.

After an extended time of routing through three different, long-distance operators, a phone began ringing in a beautiful, elegantly furnished luxury apartment in Central, Hong Kong. Thomas Chen opened his eyes and glanced at the clock on his nightstand. It was two o'clock in the morning. He reached for the phone.

Immediately switching from Mandarin to English he said, "Oh, hello Miss Anderson, yes, I can talk of course."

Thomas Chen had been expecting a call from her following their discussion several days earlier. He pulled himself to a sitting position at the side of the bed. The lights from Victoria Harbor cast a muted glow in his room. He sat and listened.

"Yes, yes, I understand," he said. "I will make the transaction in the morning. You and I will only know of this. I will move the final payment that is expected to be deposited in the current account to the new account as soon as it is transferred. I will then close the old account, and it will be deleted from the files. You can, of course, expect total discretion. I will notify you as soon as this is complete."

CHAPTER 11

Friday, December 1, 1967

"Mr. Spencer," the lady at the front desk of his hotel called out as he was passing that morning. "You received a telegram early this morning."

Spencer returned to the desk and took the telegram. "Thank you."

He stopped just outside the hotel and opened the sealed note.

It read: Today is the day. Spencer checked his watch.

He continued to the office and passed the morning reviewing outstanding investigations that were at various degrees of completion. He was mostly focused, though, on his upcoming call to Sheila. Spencer notified agent Coleman that he was running out for lunch, and at exactly 1250 hours he was standing at a phone booth several blocks down and around the corner from the Dillingham Transportation Building. A note pad and pen were sitting on the small shelf under the phone while he fished loose change out of his pocket. At two minutes until 1300 he put a dime in the phone and dialed 0. The operator answered and connected him to a long-distance operator. He inserted the required coins. At exactly 1900 hours, the phone rang in the deli in Washington DC. It was answered, again, on the first ring.

"Sheila, it's James."

Sheila responded immediately. "James let me bring you up to date quickly."

There was some static on the line so she asked, "Can you hear me, ok?"

"Yes, I can hear you." He replied.

She continued, "First, your contact for inside naval information is Zhao Li. She goes by Madam Li. She is brilliant, knows more about naval operations in the South Pacific than most of the command there, and she is completely trustworthy. She heads a very large and effective counterintelligence group in Asia. I have already notified her. She is lives in Taipei.

"Wait, spell her name."

"Z,h,a,o, and then capital Li"

"Thanks. Got it."

"Taiwan?" Spencer asked.

"Yes. You're going to be doing some traveling over the next couple of days James. She is a bit out of the way, but trust me, she is the person we need. It's not the time to be bringing in the second string."

"And that's why you're the person I need now." he replied.

"You will be meeting her in Taipei, on Monday the 4th at 1030 at a bar called the Flamingo Club & Restaurant. It's on Chungshan North Road. Are you getting all of this?"

"Flamingo Club & Restaurant, on Chungshan." He repeated.

"Yes, that's it." She replied.

"OK, thanks." Taiwan wasn't what he was hoping for, but he

was writing down the information. He had one shot at this and was not going to begin questioning any recommendations from Sheila.

"You'll pick up your tickets at the counter in Honolulu Sunday morning. You have a ticket to Taipei and then a second leg to Japan for the afternoon following your meeting with Li. And you have a return ticket back to Honolulu on Thursday evening. Is that going to give you enough time to get things sorted out in Japan?"

Spencer thought for a minute and then replied, "We'll go with those dates. If I have to, I can change the flight back to Hawaii."

"Your flight is at 1130 on Sunday. You'll be flying Japan Air Lines. You have a room booked at the Grand Hotel in Taipei for Sunday evening."

Spencer continued writing in his pad.

"I have already wired money to your bank account in Honolulu. It will be available tomorrow morning. You will need to have ten thousand US dollars in cash to give to Madam Li."

"Ten thousand? She must really be good!" Spencer interjected.

"Trust me James, it will be the best ten thousand dollars you have ever spent. And you will have more than enough for anything that might come up. You'll get to play like you're rich for a couple of days."

Spencer could sense her smile from five thousand miles away.

"I'm not going to ask what fund all of this money is coming from," Spencer replied.

Sheila laughed and said, "You have no idea the number of hidden, forgotten slush funds that are never tracked in the Bureau? It's kind of staggering. Oh, to be safe, I did empty the fund completely so that remnants of it wouldn't be found later.

There is now no record of it ever existing."

"Excellent! Have you had any luck tracking the bank account?" he asked.

"It looks like we hit the jackpot on that one James. It's just what you had suspected." Sheila then shared all the salient points from the documentation she received from Thomas Chen, and her call to the Department of the Navy.

Spencer was shocked. "A naval officer has made over sixteen million dollars selling military secrets to our enemies for years and not one person on that base has a clue. How the hell does that happen?"

"Just can't stay away from the hard ones, can you?" Sheila replied.

"Cut it out," he laughed. "You can taunt me all you want when we are in the car under the palm tree spying on people."

Sheila responded, laughing, that he might regret that statement.

"Captain William Mason, correct?" He asked.

"Yes, Captain William Mason, James."

"Sheila, you are flying under the radar, aren't you?"

"I am. Nothing to worry about on this side. I do wish I could clean out one of the other slush funds, though, and bring it with me to Hawaii. We could be spending our golden years living like royalty." Her laugh again.

They were both completely aware of the magnitude of the situation they found themselves in, and it was not a laughing matter. But being able to break the tension with a laugh is what had kept them both sane over the years.

"Again, Sheila, if this does all go south, get out immediately. If we can do anything to stop what we know is going to happen, fine. But if we can't, at least we gave it the old college try. And we'll get back on track with your move over here as soon as I get back from my adventure."

"My suitcase is already packed." She replied.

He could sense a sadness in her voice.

"Be careful James. I love you. I can't lose you now."

"I love you to Sheila, and I will be careful. You're not going to lose me." James responded softly.

They hung up their phones. Sheila walked back to her apartment, and James walked back to his office. The plan was now in motion. What happened next would affect them both for the rest of their lives.

CHAPTER 12

Navy Base Japan

Captain William Mason was leaned back in his chair with his feet planted on the desk. His hands were clasped behind his head, his eyes were closed, and he was reflecting on the future. In several months, he would be completing his tour of duty, and his thoughts were on the villa he was planning to buy in the hills outside of Umbria, Italy.

Retiring to a luxurious villa outside of Umbria, Italy isn't something one would think a Captain in the United States Navy could afford. But, over a ten-year period, William Mason had amassed a vast amount of money selling top secret United States Naval operations information to various countries that were willing to pay handsomely for it. His acquired wealth came from huge payouts from countries including the Soviet Union, North Korea, Viet Nam, and Mainland China, along with, by comparison, a small pittance from the United States Navy for his devoted years as a patriotic and respected Naval Officer.

His final outside entrepreneurial effort – enabling the delivery of United States NSA Top Secret cryptographic coding equipment to North Korea – was in place and would be completed soon. He would be meeting with Admiral Frank Johnson that afternoon to have him sign off on final procurement and readiness documents for the USS Pueblo. The, now converted spy ship was scheduled to set sail to be positioned off the coast of North Korea. Its orders were to monitor North Korean and Soviet activity. The ship had already been configured with all the necessary top secret coding equipment.

Hostile governments know that the safest way to place a spy is to rely on subversives who live within the country they are spying on. Getting a cleared person on the inside is much easier than trying to place an external spy of their own. All they must do is find that person who values his or her own interests above the interest of their country. As it turns out, it's surprisingly easy. They found a perfect fit with Captain William Mason.

A copy of the procurement requests, with specific top-secret equipment and manuals, had been wired from his largest and closest benefactor, USSR. His part of the agreement was to get Johnson to sign off on the procurement, and then to personally travel to Sasebo to make sure all the requested documents and equipment were on board before Pueblo set sail.

A ringing phone pulled him from his daydreaming. He pulled his feet off the desk, leaned forward, and picked it up.

“Captain Mason."

Mason could tell it was an outside line. The voice was muffled. “Contact 12:15; Park.” The line went dead.

The call had come from his soviet contact in Japan. Mason didn't like last minute changes, and he began to worry that there was a problem. He brushed aside that thought and pulled a file from his desk and began reading the day's logs. The morning passed by quickly. The meeting with Johnson was at 1400. Would he have time to adjust his plan if needed? There was too much riding on this plan being successful. He was anxious.

At 1145 he walked out of the building to his car and drove to a park several miles off base. The park was filled with dozens of beautiful cherry trees. The blossoms were normally gone this late in the season, but the flowers had made a rare second appearance in late September. The people who are in the know of these things said it had to do with a very active typhoon season.

The Park was abuzz with mothers pushing strollers and playing with children on the playground equipment - equipment that had been donated by the Naval Base. Mason walked to a bench facing a small pond with a fountain. He pulled a pack of Lucky Strikes from his pocket and lit a cigarette. Just then an old man with a cane stopped at his bench and sat down. He sat looking at the pond for several minutes and then slowly pulled himself to his feet and walked away. He had left a folded piece of paper on the bench. Mason continued smoking his cigarette looking at the fountain, seeming completely unaware of the old man who had just shared his bench. He then flicked the ashes from his cigarette and tossed the butt into the grass. As he stood up, he placed his hand over the folded paper and palmed it. He slipped the paper in his pocket and then drove back to the base.

Once he was back at his office, he closed the door and locked it, pulled the folded piece of paper from his pocket and returned to his desk. He slowly unfolded the paper.

The paper read:

Pueblo must go as planned. Crucial that four (4) KG-14 cryptographic machines and repair kits remain on-board They must not be unloaded as previously ordered.

No excess documents or superseded files are to be removed before ship leaves port.

Confirm no air or sea cover staged.

Mason read the paper. He wrote several notes on a notepad and then held the delivered note over his ashtray and lit it with his lighter. He watched as the last of the yellow paper dissolved into ash. He instinctively stirred the ash with a pencil.

Pulling the requisition form from his desk, he placed the last page in his typewriter and began typing. Addendum: Per intelligence, National Security Agency, the following items should be included for Pueblo preparation for departure to assigned mission.

Four (4) TSec KG-14 machines with associated manuals, and spare parts kits are to remain on-board and not removed as per earlier directive.

He pulled the page from the typewriter and put it back into the requisition document. He glanced at the clock and saw that it was 1345. Mason steeled himself and walked down the hall to the Admiral's Office.

He knocked on the door once and entered the outer office. A young seaman greeted him from behind his desk.

“Good afternoon, sir, Admiral Johnson asked that you come in as soon as you arrived."

Mason nodded and walked into Johnson's office.

The Admiral was on the phone, but as soon as he saw Mason, he motioned for him to come in and sit down. He held his hand over the phone and said, quietly, "Be done in just a second here." Johnson finished the call and hung up. "Damn, how many community things do you have to do to keep these people happy over here?" Johnson said to no one in particular.

"OK Bill, what's this whole Pueblo thing look like? Any problems at all?" Johnson asked. He always pronounced the ships’ name Pu-eb-lo, in three distinct syllables, which irritated Mason.

"I did receive a call from Intelligence, and they said there are a couple of machines that they don't want unloaded now. Apparently, they had been scheduled earlier for removal. You'll note the addendum on the last page, but other than that it looks good. That's an easy one."

"Why don't they want us to take them off?" Johnson asked.

“Have no idea why they changed their minds, and they didn't say, of course. Hey, I guess those guys are calling the shots on that secret crypto stuff," Mason chuckled. “When I talked to the guy at Intelligence, he said it was extremely important to make sure the equipment isn't removed in Sasebo as originally planned.”

“Who did you talk to in Intelligence?” Johnson inquired.

“I don't even remember. Been talking to so many of them over the past couple of weeks, I forgot who it was.”

“Well, let's get them signed so they aren't coming back bitching because we slowed things down.”

“They really can be a pain in the ass, Sir,” Mason responded, shaking his head.

"You got them there?” Johnson asked, while pointing to the folder Mason was holding in his hand.

“I do Sir.”

"Here let me just sign off on this now." Johnson signed the forms without reading them. He seldom read anything Mason asked him to sign.

So far everything was going exactly as planned.

"I'll get this information over to Captain Butcher on the change,” Mason responded,” and Intelligence wanted me to give him a list of old documents they want removed from the ship. I'll bring

Butcher up to date on the documents to remove before they sail."

"Anything else you think we need to get the Pu-eb-lo ready to set sail?" Johnson asked.

"We should be covered on everything, but I think I had better head to Sasebo, just to make sure everything goes as planned on that end. It shouldn't take me more than a couple of days. Thank you for your time, Sir"

"No problem, Bill. Hey, this ship is going to be setting off the coast of North Korea. Those crazy bastards will do anything. Is there any reason we should be looking at sea or air support in case something happens?"

"The North Koreans will be pissed, I'm sure, but they wouldn't be stupid enough to attack a United States naval vessel in international waters."

He did not use the word 'capture' for good reason.

"That's a good point Captain. The North Koreans aren't going to mess with the United States Navy. And if they do try something stupid, we should be able to get some planes in the air quick. Probably no need to get everybody riled up now trying to put planes and ships on standby for something that isn't going to happen."

Mason agreed. "We aren't going to have any problems with the North Koreans."

He stood up, picked up the file, and saluted the commander. As he turned to leave, Johnson said, "Bill, have you got time to stop by the club after work for a drink before you head to Sasebo? A couple of the guys are going to get together, and it could be a little bon voyage send off for the ship. A couple of drinks to celebrate finally getting this damn thing on its way."

Mason had plenty of reason to celebrate. "Thank you, sir. I'll be there. Save me a seat."

He held his laugh until he was out of the building. Living in the lap of luxury in a villa in Italy looked like a sure thing now. He thought for a moment how easy it was to manipulate the system. Jesus, the fact that the people running this base have lasted as long as they had was a complete mystery to Mason. But, then again, it made his job so much easier.

Mason walked back to his office and made a call to the command center for Pueblo. and asked for Butcher. Butcher picked up a line in short order.

"Butcher here."

"Captain Butcher this is Captain Mason. I'm calling to let you know you'll be keeping some of the equipment that was originally scheduled to be removed before you sailed. It's four KG-14's and their maintenance manuals. Johnson signed off on it, so guess he knows more than us."

"Shit! I don't have enough room to turn around and take a piss in here as it is now. Was looking forward to those being removed. Well, goddamn it!"

"Sorry Captain," Mason responded. "Hey, you've spent your career on subs – this should be like home for you."

They both laughed. "Ya, guess you're right, Captain." Butcher replied.

Oh, and they wanted you to wait until they got back to you on removing the old manuals and documents you still have stored on board. I know you want things cleaned up, but they assured me you'll have the list before you sail. "

"If it weren't for the constant god damned change of plans, this navy would be a great place to work," Butcher said laughing.

"Hey that's how the bigwigs keep their jobs."

"Isn't that the damn truth." Butcher replied.

“Thanks Captain Butcher. I know you guys are anxious to set sail. Oh, and sorry for being the messenger on this.”

They both hung up their phones. Mason's plan was in place and now he was going to celebrate with several drinks at the club with the guy who signed off on all of this. It was going to be a good evening.

CHAPTER 13

Thursday, January 4, 1968

It was a little after three in the afternoon when Spencer landed in Taipei. He maneuvered through the terminal and found ground transportation. He was glad to see that there was a short queue to hire a cab. He walked to the next available one and got in, closing the door behind him. He gave the driver the name of the hotel and sat back. Other than a few quick maneuvers, some horn blowing and what Spencer suspected to be cursing from the driver he arrived at his hotel in due time, unscathed.

The cab pulled to a stop under the ornately decorated, red pillared Porte-cochere of the Chi-Lin Pavilion of the Grand Hotel in Taipei. He had just paid the driver when a doorman stepped to the vehicle and opened the back door. Spencer exited the cab, took several steps up to the large, equally ornate entrance doors and entered the lobby.

By the looks of the hotel, he suspected that Sheila must have cleaned out one of the largest slush funds in the bureau.

He walked to the registration desk and was greeted by a sharply dressed clerk.

"Good afternoon, Sir. How may I help you?"

"My name is James Spencer, and I have a reservation for this evening."

The sharply dressed clerk stepped back and pulled several pieces of paper from below the desk.

"Thank you for staying with us, Mr. Spencer. I see that your bill has already been handled. I hope you have a wonderful stay. The restaurant and bar are just there to the left and room service is available twenty-four hours a day. If you have any special requests, please feel free to call the front desk at any hour."

Spencer thanked him, took his key and headed to the elevators. He had already decided that he would not be coming back down to the lobby or restaurant until he checked out the following morning. Having an envelope in your briefcase filled with ten thousand dollars in hundred-dollar bills would dictate close watching and keeping it with you in a locked hotel room would certainly improve the chances of it staying in place.

He hadn't had a chance to eat since a quick bite at the airport in Hawaii that morning, and flight turbulence made eating on the plane a bit too much of a challenge. He stuck with Scotch and a splash of water. As a result, room service was at the top of his list. He unlocked his room door and stepped in, double checking the lock as he closed it behind him. He sat his briefcase and carry-on bag on the bed and surveyed his surroundings. It was a large room with an attached sitting area with a couch and several overstuffed chairs that overlooked the hectic commotion of the crowds and traffic on the street below. A table and two chairs were positioned between the sitting room and the bedroom The rooms were beautifully adorned.

The phone was sitting on a stand to the right of the bed, closest to the sitting room. Spencer walked around the bed, picked up the phone and rang room service. His call was answered immediately. He placed his order and hung up.

He then noticed a small TV setting on a chest of drawers across from the foot of the bed. Not knowing what to expect, he turned it on and waited. He was surprised when he heard the theme song for Cheyenne – an American western. He found it odd that he was in a hotel room in Taipei, Republic of China watching Cheyenne Bodie ride into the screen, and even a bit odder when Clint Walker moseyed his horse up to the sheriff's office, slowly dismounted, and then spoke to the sheriff in Mandarin. He stood watching for several minutes and then sat on the bed focused on the screen until room service knocked on the door to announce his dinner had arrived.

The dinner as it turned out was delicious. He sipped his scotch, ate a perfectly prepared steak, and continued his TV watching from the table. After several game shows that seemed vaguely familiar to shows in the states, he shut off the tv, showered, brushed his teeth and went to bed. He slept surprisingly well.

The following morning, he dressed, removed the envelope with the ten thousand dollars from his briefcase, put it in his jacket pocket and walked down to the restaurant. His breakfast, again, reflected the five-star moniker of the Grand Hotel. It was delicious. He was thankful Sheila had handled his trip arrangements. Had they been handled by his scheduler at the WFO he would have been watching a broken neon light flashing outside the cracked window of an eight-by-ten dump.

Following breakfast, Spencer checked out of the hotel and walked out the front door where he was immediately greeted by another well-groomed gentleman who quickly flagged a cab. Spencer gave the cab driver the name of the club and the address as best he could and hoped that he had understood. The driver straightaway pulled from the hotel and drove with a determined demeanor, so Spencer sat back with a somewhat confident feeling that he would reach his destination.

In about 10 minutes the cab pulled to the curb and stopped. Without looking back, the driver said, "Flamingo Club. Pay now."

Spencer paid for the ride and stepped out of the cab. Chungshan North was a busy 4 lane road with wide sidewalks lined with shops, bars and occasional trees. He turned and saw that he was standing in front of an establishment with a sign above the windows that read Florida Bakery. Having put his trust in the fact that the driver knew where he was going, he walked to the corner of the building at Nung An Street and spotted the sign for the Flamingo Club pointing up a flight of stairs. The club was above the bakery.

Spencer looked at his watch. It was 1020. He opened the door to the club and climbed the stairs, entering an almost empty establishment. A Wurlitzer Jukebox at the far end of the room, near the bar, was quietly playing *'It's Now or Never'.*

After his Cheyenne awakening from the night before, he wasn't surprised. But still, walking into a club in Taipei and being greeted by Elvis seemed somewhat surreal.

The bar was a bit stuffy, and smelled of alcohol, accented with a lingering hint of perfume worn by the girls who were working the night before.

Once his eyes had adjusted to the dim light, he noticed a well-dressed lady sitting with a man at a small corner table. The lady looked up and nodded slightly. As he approached the table, she said something to her companion who then moved to the bar. She looked up at Spencer and motioned for him to come closer.

"You are Agent Spencer?" she questioned.

"I am. Thank you for meeting with me Madam Li."

Zhao Li nodded and said, "Welcome to Taiwan Agent Spencer. Please be seated."

She was a small lady. Spencer guessed her to be about sixty, but that was just a guess at best. She was impeccably dressed, wearing a black silk flowered dress with a mandarin collar. Her stunning diamond earrings and necklace would turn the head of royalty - he had no doubts the jewelry was authentic. Her hair was pulled back into a neat bun, her designer purse was sitting on the table, and her hands were clasped together resting in front of her. She looked slowly around the club. Satisfied that they were not being watched, she began.

"We can talk safely here. Your contact in Washington has informed me that you need information on certain naval operations and personnel in Japan."

Before Spencer could reply, she asked, "You have the money of course?"

Spencer reached into his inside jacket pocket, removed the stuffed white envelope and slid it across the table to Li. She picked up the envelope and put it into her purse without counting it.

She spoke quietly. "I understand you are looking for information on an individual at the Yokosuka Naval Base in Japan, and a ship called Pueblo."

"Yes, I am looking for information on both." Spencer responded.

She continued, still in a hushed voice. "The ship Pueblo is now docked at the base in Yokosuka. It will be leaving port tomorrow morning for the U.S. Naval base in Sasebo, Japan. The stop at Sasebo will be for replenishment & final fitting. They will be unloading several of the secret cryptographic machines and any excess documents that are not required for the deployment. It will leave Sasebo on January 11, headed through the Tsushima Strait toward the Sea of Japan and finally to North Korea. The ship will be positioned near the port of Wonsan. Their mission is to monitor North Korean and Soviet Naval activity and intercept communications transmissions."

"Your knowledge of the Pueblo is surprising Madam Li." Spencer responded.

"Not as surprising as you might think, Agent Spencer. You see, everything that I have just shared comes from several well-placed waiters at the officers' club at the naval base in Yokosuka."

"You have to be kidding," Spencer replied.

"No, it is true. It seems that after several drinks, your military officers tend to openly share their exploits with the other top brass around the table. I believe 'Loose lips sink ships' is no longer a directive in your Navy. It appears that your many enemies' most effective espionage technique could be nothing more than a couple of martinis."

She looked at Spencer directly. "We are, as you say, the good guy's Agent Spencer. But you understand we are not the only ones serving drinks at club."

Li continued. "I can share one other important piece of information Agent Spencer. Your government had contacted me two months ago to validate the possibility that the North Koreans were being supplied with top secret documentation and schematics for a submarine tracking system called SOSUS. If their suspicions were true, it was crucial that the supplier was found and eliminated.

One of my top agents, who was embedded in the North Korean Navy, had been gathering information on SOSUS. His last message to us was that the Koreans were buying the top-secret information from a well-positioned United States Naval Officer stationed in Yokosuka. Unfortunately, it was our last report, and we were to find out later that this agent was brutally tortured and murdered in an abandoned building outside of Ch'aho Naval Base. The torture and murder were witnessed by another agent of ours who was most certainly unable to intervene for risk of being killed also."

"Madam Li, the man I am looking for is a Captain William Mason. We believe he is planning to provide the Soviets with United States top secret cryptographic coding equipment. Do you have any information as to the name of the Naval Officer who is selling information on the SOSUS?" Spencer asked.

"No, I do not. The agent who witnessed the murder was evacuated from Korea and is now back in Japan. He has told us that the man who directed the interrogation, torture and murder was an American. He was there while the skin was sectioned and pealed from the agents' body while he was still alive, begging to be shot. No, he did not have a name, but the voice and look of this American's face are permanently etched into his memory."

"My god! I can't imagine." Spencer replied.

Madam Li continued, "It would seem highly unlikely that two different naval officers from the same base are involved in espionage at this level. It appears, Agent Spencer, that we are both looking for the same man."

Spencer now understood why Sheila directed him to Madam Li.

"Agent Spencer, the Chinese have a word called Fuchou. It means to avenge. My personal interest in this butcher now is Fuchou. We are a rather large organization, as you have come to learn Agent Spencer. We have people imbedded in many countries. My people are at risk every day as they dedicate their lives to this dark business of espionage, and they accept that, but no one should ever be faced with what our agent in North Korea endured. My only focus on this man is to see that he pays dearly for what he did."

"Agent Spencer, because it seems we both now have a vested

interest in capturing this man, I would like to ask that one of our agents work with you while you are in Japan. He has Korean heritage on his mother's side, but his father is Japanese. He understands the country, the people, the language and the customs. He will most certainly be valuable in helping you conduct your search, and you ours.

Spencer understood the limitations he faced working in Japan. The addition of Madam Li's man would, in fact, be extremely valuable.

"Under the circumstances, I can see how it would make sense to work as a team." Spencer replied. "Yes, of course. We should work together."

"Do you believe you will find this Naval Officer in Yokosuka, Agent Spencer?" She asked.

"I honestly don't know, but I believe it is where we must start."

"In that case, we should begin there." She added.

"How will I find your agent?" Spencer inquired.

"He will contact you in Japan. His name is Sato Katashi."

Spencer repeated the name.

"I hope that our meeting today has been helpful Agent Spencer."

"It most certainly has; Madam Li. Thank you.

"Be very careful Agent Spencer. These men are animals."

Spencer nodded, stood, and walked out of the club. His mind was now focused on the plane he had to catch to Tokyo.

He stepped to the curb and waved a cab.

"Airport please." The car pulled away and maneuvered into the chaotic traffic.

CHAPTER 14

Yokosuka Japan
January 4, 1968

Spencer's plane touched down in Tokyo at 1515. A short cab ride found him at the train station purchasing a ticket for the next train to Yokosuka. He was fortunate that the train had arrived just minutes earlier, leaving him sufficient time to board before it departed. He walked to his first-class car and stepped onto the train.

The carriage was sparsely occupied. He found a seat toward the back of the car, away from the other passengers, and settled in. It was then that he began to seriously question his decision to try and find Mason and stop the Pueblo from sailing. He realized that he had no plan in place other than that he had to try and do something. He was fully aware that his chances of finding this man and stopping the ship from sailing were probably nothing more than wishful thinking. But Spencer was very capable of compartmentalizing any doubts and locking them away. That compartment would not be opened again. He would move forward.

The train ride to Yokosuka was scheduled to take an hour and fourteen minutes. He glanced briefly out the window at the activity of people scurrying about on the platform and then reached for a magazine in the wall rack next to his seat. The magazine was in Japanese. He quickly flipped through the pages and then returned it to the holder. The train began to slowly pull out of the station.

It was just then that a casually, but well-dressed gentleman of Japanese descent walked down the aisle of his car and stopped next to the two seats facing Spencer.

"Might I join you?" the man asked.

Spencer questioned why he hadn't chosen one of the many empty seats toward the front of the car. While it seemed unlikely that Madam Li's contact could have found him so quickly, it was possible that he had underestimated their skill. His English was excellent. Spencer sensed a slight, almost British accent.

"Of course, please." Spencer replied, lifting his arm to acknowledge the two empty seats across from him.

The man removed a leather satchel that had been strapped across his shoulder and placed it on the seat. He then sat down in the seat directly across from Spencer. They visually acknowledged each other as the new passenger nodded slightly.

"Mr. Spencer, my name is Sato Katashi. I believe we will be working together for the next few days."

"I am impressed that you have found me so quickly, Mr. Sato." Spencer replied.

"We have valuable sources of information in Japan, Mr. Spencer. Your cab driver to the station is one of them." Sato said, smiling.

"It is very nice to meet you Mr. Sato. And yes, it appears that we will be working together. I understand that we may be looking for the same man – although for different reasons."

"That is my belief also," Sato replied, "and I understand that you are under serious time constraints, Mr. Spencer. Perhaps our best plan at this point is to share with each other everything that we can about the man we are each searching for."

"You are correct Mr. Sato, I am under serious time constraints, and I am happy to share everything I can. We are not in a position to slowly earn each other's trust before we begin. We do not have the time. We will have to assume."

Sato casually crossed his legs and folded his hands in his lap. Spencer was impressed with the calmness that Sato displayed. It was obvious he wasn't one to be rattled easily.

"I am looking for a man named William Mason," Spencer began. "Have you heard that name mentioned before?"

"William Mason, no, I have not." Sato replied.

"Our information is that he is a Naval Captain stationed at the Yokosuka Naval Base."

Sato responded again that he was not familiar with the name.

"We know that the man we are looking for has been selling secret government information to several foreign countries. And we believe that he is involved in the deployment of a government spy ship."

Their conversation was as hushed as possible considering the rumbling of the train.

Spencer continued, "We know that the ship is scheduled to be positioned off the coast of North Korea for surveillance of North Korean and Soviet naval shipping activity. The ship will be fitted with top secret cryptographic equipment that is of interest to the USSR. It is our feeling that the ship will be captured by the North Korean's, and the equipment will be confiscated. Stopping this man, and the sailing of the ship is of the utmost urgency."

Sato remained cross legged and calm as he responded. "I understand that Madam Li has shared with you our interest in finding this man, Mr. Spencer."

"She has."

Spencer leaned forward a bit and lowered his voice. "Perhaps she has told you that I am working outside the constraints of the FBI. My contact, in Washington, and I, are the only two people who know of my presence in Taiwan and Japan."

Sato casually uncrossed his legs and leaned forward a bit himself. "Madam Li did share with me the situation you find yourself in Mr. Spencer. She felt my understanding of this was very important."

Spencer continued. "I'm not sure how much she could share, but I was transferred from Washington to Hawaii because the FBI wanted to stop me from investigating a naval spy who is selling top secret cryptographic codes to the Soviet Embassy in Washington. It would have been 'inconvenient' for our government if information of the spy got out, so I was pulled from the investigation and transferred to Hawaii. If any word of my involvement in a case that could be directly or even indirectly related to the naval spy in Washington, I would be considered a rogue agent and targeted."

"Certainly not a position one would want to find oneself in." Sato responded

"At this point, Mr. Sato, my interest in finding this man is almost as personal as yours."

Sato's expression defined his understanding.

"What will you do with the Naval Officer when you find him, Mr. Spencer."

"That, sir, is a very good question. My hope is to interrogate him for any information on the Pueblo and ascertain any path to stopping the ship from sailing. If we can't stop the ship from leaving port, this man will have to be stopped none the less."

"And because of the position you find yourself in, you will be unable to arrest the man and present him to authorities?" Sato added.

"That is correct Mr. Sato. I can't use any of the information he shares against him because my involvement would be discovered immediately, and my days would be numbered."

The train continued to rumble and sway gently as it traveled through the Japanese countryside.

"Mr. Spencer, I have spoken with Madam Li and she has asked me to present the possibility of handing this man over to us after you speak with him. This of course would be contingent on him being the man we are both looking for."

Spencer did not answer immediately.

"I believe that putting him in our custody, Mr. Spencer, could very easily be the perfect solution to many of the problems we are both faced with. You will know that he has been stopped, and we will have the man we most desperately want. And you, you Mr. Spencer, will remain hidden from all of this."

Spencer thought quietly for a moment, as a distant train whistle seemed to accentuate the meaning of what was just said.

"Not only does it sound like an excellent solution, Mr. Sato," Spencer replied, "but it could, in fact, be our only solution. Yes, if this does happen to be the man that we are both looking for, I will turn him over to you after I speak with him.

It was then that a hostess stopped with a small cart and offered a sandwich, a drink and a damp, heated towel. They both accepted the sandwich and towel. Spencer opted for a double Scotch while Sato asked for a Seagram's and a can of coke. They thanked her and she again moved toward the front of the car. The two men continued their discussion.

"We still have a big question that must be answered." Spencer began. "We still don't know if we are both talking about the same man."

"We can only answer that for sure if we find him." Sato concluded.

The train was now 45 minutes from Yokosuka. They both ate their sandwiches, wiped their hands and faces with the hot, damp towel, and lifted their beautifully etched crystal glasses of liquor. Holding their drinks, they toasted the eventual success of their mission.

"Mr. Sato, where would one search for a Naval Officer in Japan, off of the base of course?" Spencer asked.

"I believe I know of a place we might start." Sato responded. "There is an area in Yokosuka called bar town. It is where the US Navy seaman from the Naval Base go to throw away their pay when they are off duty. There are two bars, Bar Betty and New Tokyo that are regularly the most visited by navy personnel. Visiting a busy bar with inebriated sailors might be a good spot to start. And it will put us near the ship you are looking for. Someone might happen to share enough information to give us some direction in our search.

"Very good, Mr. Sato. Bar Betty and New Tokyo will be our first stops."

Sato nodded his head in agreement. and then reached for the satchel in the seat next to him and placed it on his lap.

"Agent Spencer, are you familiar with the Nambu Type 94 Service Pistol?"

"I am not?"

Sato removed a wrapped package from his satchel and handed it to Spencer.

Spencer unwrapped the package, a Nambu pistol, and held the gun in his hand.

"You will be in need of protection while you are in Japan," Mr. Spencer, "and an unmarked, untraceable weapon is of preference. There are thousands of Nambu handguns available on the black market in Japan making them the perfect choice for us. We will both have one in our possession.

"Makes sense. What do I need to know about this Nambu."

"It is an 8mm Japanese pistol that hasn't been in production for years. It is recoil operated, locked breech, and has a magazine capacity of 8 rounds. It is not the easiest weapon to handle because, as I'm sure you have already noticed, it has a very small grip."

Spencer was holding the weapon in his hand to get a feel of it.

Sato continued, "You are not going to hit a moving target at fifty yards, but it is very useful at close range. And half of the thugs in Japan use them, so they can never be traced back to us."

Spencer was checking to see if the gun was loaded while responding, "The grip is small, but I can deal with it."

Sato removed a second magazine from the satchel and handed it to Spencer. "I have another dozen or so bullets if the need arises."

Spencer placed the pistol and magazine in his jacket pocket.

They finished their journey in silence. Both reflecting internally on the near future.

The train arrived at the Yokosuka train station at about 3:45. Sato suggested that they secure Spencer's brief case and carry on in a locked storage locker at the station, which they did.

Spencer followed Sato thru the train station to ground transportation. The cab ride to bar town took less than ten minutes.

CHAPTER 15

Bar in Yokosuka - Bar Betty

It was four thirty in the afternoon when Spencer and Sato walked into Bar Betty. It was already half full. By the haircuts and sophomoric antics of most of the patrons, it wasn't a far stretch to surmise they were young, enlisted navy personnel.

The two men found an empty table with four chairs setting near a grouping of several tables that had been pushed together and were occupied with about a dozen, noisy sailors. As Spencer and Sato sat down, two young, attractive bargirls appeared out of nowhere and took a seat in the two other empty chairs at their table. "You want company? You buy drink?"

Sato looked at Spencer and said, "We will buy these girls drinks. We need them with us, so we don't stand out."

Sato turned to the girls and said, smiling, "We buy drinks." It was one of the few times that Spencer had seen him smile since they first met.

"We take Mai Tai."

Sato ordered a scotch for Spencer, a Seagram's and coke for

himself, and two Mai Tai's.

The waitress arrived with the drinks and placed them on the table. The girls grabbed theirs immediately and began drinking. The girls in the bars in bar town were paid tips by the bar for each drink they were bought. There was no alcohol in the fancy concoctions, and they were the most expensive drinks at the table.

The girls sat sipping their soft drinks and talking between themselves, giggling occasionally.

The group of young sailors in the next table had obviously been there for some time. Spencer wondered how in the hell they were going to get back to base in their condition.

"Did you hear that?" Sato asked.

"What?"

Sato nodded his head toward the table beside them. "They mentioned 'Pueblo'."

"You're kidding."

They listened and Spencer also heard the name Pueblo mentioned.

They sat back in their chairs and focused on the conversation of the loud group of sailors surrounding the pushed together tables next to theirs. It became obvious that the inebriated young men, many with girls on their laps, were assigned to the Pueblo, and were talking, openly, about shipping out the next morning to Sasebo. They were also talking about it being a secret mission and they didn't know where they were ultimately headed.

One of the girls, who was wrapped around a smiling sailor said, "You on Pueblo? Spy ship. You guys very important. You like James Bond?"

One of the sailors responded that maybe they were like James

Bond. But they couldn't tell the girls about anything they did, or they would have to kill them.

The girls caught the essence of their joke but were undeterred.

"You know Captain Billy?" one of the other girls asked.

They looked at the girl and said, "Who is Captain Billy?"

"You don't know? He very big shot and big spender. Not like you."

A girl in a short green dress, sitting on the lap of another sailor said, "He big shot in Navy in Japan."

The sailors at the table all denied knowing him.

The girl in the green dress continued. "He at bar last night, buy plenty drinks. He go Sasebo today. He in charge everything about Pueblo."

"Hey, how do you girls know so much about the Pueblo?" one of them asked.

"We know about Pueblo. You go North Korea."

Spencer thought to himself, "Jesus Christ, every bargirl in here knows where the secret Navy spy ship is going! How the hell did we ever win any wars?"

"Didn't you say that the man you are looking for is a Captain Mason?" Sato asked

"Yes, Mason," Spencer responded.

Sato continued, "A Captain William Mason… Captain Billy?"

"Jesus Christ! There is no way we can be this lucky." Spencer replied. "But it does make total sense!"

The girls sitting with Spencer and Sato were, by now, aware that the two men they were with were not interested in talking with them. It didn't matter, because the tips from the drinks were very good, so they were happy to just sit talking and giggling between themselves.

The girl setting closest to Sato reached over and touched his arm. “You buy more drink?” He smiled slightly and nodded his head yes. The girl held up her empty glass and yelled to the bar tender, “Two Mai Tai!”

Spencer then continued, “According to Madam Li, the Pueblo would be making the stop at Sasebo to load additional equipment and documents. It would make sense that Captain Mason would be headed there early to coordinate the loading.”

Sato nodded his head in agreement

“But the only thing we know is that there is someone called Captain Billy who, according to the girls here in Bar Betty, is a big shot who knows everything about the Pueblo - and he is going to Sasebo. Not a hell of a lot to go on, but it is our best lead right now.”

They decided that their next stop would be Sasebo. Sato said that the fastest way to get there was by plane, but it was a route that was usually booked ahead, and it probably wouldn’t be possible to get tickets for several days. The other option was the train. It was a nine-hour trip, but it was their fastest option. The two men left Bar Betty, leaving the girls and numerous inebriated young sailors who were going to wake up the next morning in their bunks wondering what happened to all of their money.

They found that the next train to Sasebo was leaving the next morning at 0730. They purchased their first class, tickets for the next morning, picked up Spencer’s brief case and carry on from the locker and found a hotel for the evening. As soon as they got booked into the hotel, they headed to a restaurant that was just across the street.

They had dinner, neither mentioning their mission. They then headed back to their rooms to hopefully get a night's sleep. It was going to be long next day.

CHAPTER 16

January 5, 1968

The nine-hour train ride from Yokosuka to Sasebo gave them a bit of down time. Neither Spencer nor Sato were of the nature to share information about their personal lives, but they had developed a slightly closer bond over the past day, and the ride gave them the opportunity to get to know each other a bit better - albeit perhaps just very small snippets.

They reviewed their mutual interest in the man they were seeking. The man that they both agreed was most likely the same person.

They also recapped their visit to Bar Betty in Yokosuka the evening before, recalling a discussion that the girls had begun about how Captain Billy had told them that they were all prettier than the girls in the bars in Sasebo. It seemed to be a comment that the girls were all in agreement with.

It was then that one of the sailors, who seemed to be familiar with the drinking holes in Sasebo had asked, "Oh Yah! What bars in Sasebo?"

The girls, each trying to speak over the others yelled several names. They then settled on 'all the bars in Paradise Alley'.

"Wait, didn't they say Mason mentioned a Club Rainbow?" Spencer asked.

"Yes, it was Club Rainbow." Sato responded.

The two made the somewhat obvious assumption that if Captain Mason frequented the bars in Yokosuka, it wouldn't be too far of a stretch to assume he knew the bars in Sasebo quite well also. If he mentioned Club Rainbow, then that was where they would begin.

They also agreed that, unfortunately, the most reliable source for information in Japan, so far, had been bar girls in Yokosuka.

"I still can't believe this," Spencer added. "Every bar girl at the club had knowledge of a secret United States, spy ship sailing from Japan to North Korea." He wondered again how we had won any wars.

Sato listened but didn't respond.

The train finally came to a noisy, clanking, squealing, steam belching stop at the Sasebo train station. Spencer grabbed his briefcase and overnight bag as Sato strapped his satchel over his shoulder, and they joined the queue leaving the carriage. The train station was a sea of activity as hundreds of people headed in different directions.

Spencer and Sato had managed to get some sleep on the train, so they passed on looking for a hotel and, instead, locked Spencer's briefcase and bag in a locker at the station and then grabbed a cab to paradise alley.

"Club Rainbow," Sato told the driver.

"You go Bar Town. Good time for sure," the driver replied.

As the cab pulled out, Spencer leaned over and with a silenced voice said to Sato, "He's going to be in Sasebo at least until the Pueblo sails. Let's hope we're right, and he likes to spend his nights in the bars. I just hope to hell this isn't a wild goose chase. We've got to find this son-of-a-bitch."

After some harrowing traffic maneuvers, the cab pulled to a stop at the end of a narrow road filled on both sides with bars and clubs.

"Club Rainbow," the driver said, pointing out his window down the road. "Bar Town. Paradise Alley. You have good time Club Rainbow," he said nodding. "All navy guys go there."

Spencer paid the driver, and they got out. The conglomeration of signs that beckoned off duty sailors covered both sides of the road. It was an impressive display of establishments whose business plans were built around emptying the wallets of lonely sailors ready to party.

Spencer was first to speak. "Before we head to the bar, let's look around. If we run into this guy, we'll need to have someplace to take him to talk. Setting in a bar probably wouldn't be conducive to the line of questioning I have in mind."

Sato agreed.

Spencer continued, "I saw something from the cab that might work out." He pointed back up the street. "Just up there to the right."

When they were driving in, he had noticed a small access road, or alley that ran between the buildings. It was just wide enough for one vehicle to traverse but easily provided access for pedestrians who once visited the few now empty shops on either side.

"Here, let's check this out," he said.

They turned down the alley and walked about fifteen yards until they came across an abandoned store front that looked like it might have once been a laundry. Spencer looked back down the alley toward the main road and saw no one. The door to the empty building was slightly open. Spencer pushed the door. It required a bit of effort, but it opened, and they walked in. The only light in the room was coming through the filthy window that faced the alley. It took a few minutes to get accustomed to the dark. Once they did, they found themselves in a room filled with litter and empty boxes. An open door off the main room led to another room that appeared to be better lit. They stepped into the smaller room and saw that neon lights from the adjoining building were positioned directly over a skylight in the ceiling, providing enough light for their purposes. There were several chairs scattered about, but other than that the room was empty. The deserted store was secluded and out of the way. They would use it.

They walked back to Paradise Alley and maneuvered through the throngs of hopeful sailors. They stopped momentarily in front of Club Rainbow, but Spencer motioned Sato to follow him across the street. "Let's stop in here first."

The sign above the establishment said, Stand Bar, Three Seven. They walked in, moved toward the bar, and ordered two drinks. Glancing around, they found an empty, tall round table near the front window and positioned themselves. It would be a good spot to review their plan.

"Let's hope the bargirls were right," Sato reflected.

"My votes on the girls," Spencer said, smiling. "It kind of has to be."

"Look, we've got several days before the Pueblo pulls into port here, but I can't see us spending days sitting in bars hoping he shows up. The more I think about it, this plan leaves a lot to be desired. Christ, let's just pray we get lucky."

Sato shared one of his rare smiles, "My votes on the girls." And then with a more serious look said, "And my guess is our man plans to spend several days hitting the bars before the Pueblo arrives. I don't think he will pass up any opportunity to impress the throngs."

Spencer gave a slight nod and said, "You know, you're probably right. So, let's just assume we beat the odds, and we do run into this son-of-a-bitch. There's a good chance he won't be alone. Things could get dicey quick, and we're only going to have one chance to grab him, so let's don't screw this up."

"We've both been after him too long to let things fall apart now." Sato responded. No smile this time.

Spencer continued, "We'll need to get him out of the bar with as little commotion as possible, and back to the laundry. I'll go into the club alone. You wait here and then follow in a few minutes. I will try to find a seat at the bar. Find a seat away from me, but within view. If I find him, I'll get him out of the bar. You stay behind for a few minutes after we leave to see if we are being followed. I need you to be covering my back. If someone does follow us your job will be to stop him. Whatever the case, we meet at the laundry. Oh, and we use the Nambu's."

As he turned to leave, Sato said, "Let's hope this is the night. Be careful."

Spencer crossed the narrow street and entered Club Rainbow. He walked toward the far end of the bar, ignoring the advances from several bargirls, and found a stool facing the front door. He ordered a Scotch and causally observed the room while he waited. Several minutes later Sato walked in the front door of the club and took a seat at the opposite end of the bar. He had an unobstructed view of Spencer.

They made no eye contact while they waited. Sato had ordered his drink and was monitoring the activity in the room. Spencer continued sitting at the bar, appearing to be contemplating his glass of whisky.

Within fifteen minutes two men walked into the club. The well-dressed man in front wore slim-fit trousers, a button-down, fitted, shirt with two buttons opened at the top, and a patterned sport coat. He looked accomplished, comfortable and very sure of himself. His heavy gold necklace was accented by the expensive gold Rolex on his left wrist.

Spencer also noticed that he was armed with a handgun in a shoulder holster on his left side.

And then the second man came into view. Spencer was surprised to see that it was Francis Curry. His last sighting of Curry was at the La Paloma bar when he was buying Heineken beer for the customers.

The evening was looking like it might turn out even better than he and Sato had hoped.

Spencer knew that Curry was involved in this Pueblo plot but had assumed that his involvement was working outside the inner circle. Apparently, he was more directly involved. A holstered handgun was also strapped to his left shoulder under his jacket.

Spencer's gut told him that the first man had to be Mason, but he still needed a positive identification. He was going to move forward with the assumption that he was and plan accordingly.

The two men chatted with a few of the bargirls as they walked toward the back of the bar. A girl who was sitting on a sailor's lap several tables away from the two men, waved and yelled. "Captain Billy!" He nodded, slightly in her direction.

They continued toward the bar and took the two empty seats directly next to Spencer.

Not believing his luck, Spencer continued to slowly spin his glass while seeming completely unaware of anything going on around him.

He realized that from this point on, the plan was going to be all off script. He glanced briefly at Sato and nodded his head slightly toward the two men at the bar next to him. Sato acknowledged the message.

As the two men talked, Spencer began to reflect on what he was about to do. He was going to kidnap a highly decorated United States military officer and interrogate him. And he was somehow going to make sure that his days in the military and as a spy were over.

He had already come to grips with the fact his career in the bureau had come to an end. If he lived through the next couple of days, or didn't get arrested, he would probably stay on until he could retire with his pension, but it was no longer a valued career. It was just a job, nothing more.

Once he had realized that his blind faith and naiveté, for all those years, had hidden an actual corrupt underbelly to the institution that he had dedicated his life and career to, it made his next decisions much easier. The Bureau had stopped him from apprehending a spy in Norfolk, Virginia, and he would most likely not have the means to stop a United States Naval Vessel filled with top secret cryptographic equipment from being hand delivered to the North Koreans, but there was still this one thing he could do. He could stop Mason and Curry. These two despicable pieces of crap had to be stopped that evening.

Spencer knew this would be his last hurrah. If he and Sato did manage to stop these two, he certainly wasn't going to be rewarded with another fancy commendation from the Bureau to hang on his wall. If this went off as planned, they would never know of his involvement in any of this.

It seemed like the perfect way to end his career.

As Spencer took a sip of scotch, he heard Curry tell Mason, "I've got to take a piss." Curry stood up, but before he headed to the men's room, he rapped his knuckles on the bar and yelled, "Hey Yuto my man, two more here."

The bartender gave him thumbs up and Curry headed to the bathroom at the back of the bar.

Spencer waited until the men's room door closed and then stood up and moved directly behind Mason.

"Mr. Mason?"

Mason didn't turn to acknowledge Spencer. He stayed seated, facing the bar, and said, "That's Captain Mason. Who wants to know?"

Spencer thought to himself that that couldn't have been easier.

He moved in closer and spoke. "I have a gun pointed at your back Captain Mason. You are going to quietly stand up and walk out the door in front of me." He pushed the barrel of his Smith and Wesson into Mason's ribs.

Mason turned slightly to try and look at the man holding a gun in his back, and said, "Do you realize you are talking to a decorated officer in the United States Navy, you asshole?"

The cocky attitude of the decorated officer didn't help his cause.

The weight of the blued carbon steel Combat Magnum slamming into Mason's side might have had something to do with what sounded like a snapped rib. But Spencer's pent-up anger from over the past few weeks, was probably the bigger catalyst. Mason yelled out in pain, but his outburst was lost in the noise of the packed bar. While Mason was trying to breath, Spencer took the opportunity to reach under his jacket and remove his gun. The bartender glanced back for a second but then returned to pouring drinks. No one else noticed. The severe pain did manage to get Mason's attention though. He immediately stood up and walked toward the door. Spencer was directly behind him, the barrel of his gun intermittently jabbing his, now, very sore, ribs.

As they walked out of the bar, Spencer said, "When we get out the door, turn right and keep walking. And if you say one word, your buddy is going to come out and find your decorated ass dead on the street. Capiche?"

Mason nodded and continued walking.

As they walked past Sato, Spencer glanced at him and mouthed the word 'danger' while nodding his head toward the men's room. Sato shook his head in acknowledgement. He then picked up his drink and turned his attention to the men's room door in the back of the room.

Within 30 seconds Curry came out of the men's room and headed toward the bar. Sato noticed him tense when he saw Mason wasn't there. Curry looked around the room thinking he might have been distracted by one of the bargirls, but he didn't see him.

"Hey Yuto, where's Mason?"

"He just walked out with another guy."

Curry motioned for the bartender to follow him. They stopped just outside the front door of the bar; Curry telling Yuto to go down the road to the left while he turned toward the right.

Sato followed the two men to the front door and turned right, following Curry.

Curry stopped briefly at the bar next to Club Rainbow and glanced in. Sato could see that he had a panicked look on his face. He could also see that he was holding his handgun in his right hand, hiding it in the sleeve of his jacket. Sato looked back and saw the bartender, who was now about half a block down the road, disappearing into a crowd of sailors.

Sato lost sight of Curry briefly as a group of sailors convened to block his view. Once he caught sight of him again, Sato saw Curry was turning right at the main street - headed directly toward the ally where Spencer was taking Mason. Sato stopped at the main street and carefully looked around the corner.

"Kuso," Sato blurted as he saw Curry turn down the alley where the disserted laundry was – the laundry where Spencer and Mason now were.

He began running and reached the ally just in time to see Curry stop in front of the laundry. He seemed to be looking at the floor beneath the door to the empty shop. Sato realized that there was most likely an area where the dirt and dust had been wiped when Spencer had opened the door earlier. The man, now with his gun in his hand in full view, walked into the dark empty laundry. Sato realized that he didn't have much time.

He walked as fast and quietly as he could and stopped just before the laundry door. His Nambu was in his hand as he listened and then peeked around the corner of the door. He could just make out Curry standing near the door to the smaller office. He was faintly visible in the dim glow from the skylight, holding his handgun and peering around the door into the smaller room.

Even in the cold air, Sato could feel that he was perspiring. He was aiming his weapon at the accomplice, ready to take a shot. The empty laundry remained silent.

It was then that he sensed movement directly behind him. The angled window at the doorway reflected a man sneaking up with his pistol drawn. His training and reflexes took over.

It takes 35 pounds of sharp pressure to fracture tracheal cartilage. Immobilization is immediate and death of strangulation can occur in less than five minutes. Sato understood the mechanics of crushing someone's windpipe.

The roundhouse kick landed on the front of the bartender's throat. The bartender dropped to the ground. Curry, hearing the noise at the front door of the laundry, turned and fired. Sato heard the bullet fly past his head. Unfortunately for Curry, the movement placed him in view of Spencer. But realizing that Spenser probably couldn't see who was silhouetted at the doorway, he immediately yelled out, "James, I'm in the ally!" Another bullet hit the door jamb within inches of Sato's head.

Just then a bright flash lit up the small room followed immediately by the near deafening discharge of Spencer's Nambu. Sato watched Curry collapse to the floor.

"Spencer, you good?" Sato yelled.

"Good in here. You hit?"

"No." Sato yelled back. "Hang on a second; let me check the guy I just kicked."

"What guy you just kicked?" Spencer yelled back.

"The bartender."

After a few seconds Sato responded, "He's alive, but barely. I'm thinking we may want to find somewhere else to be really quick!"

Mason walked out of the small room in front of Spencer. They both had to step over Curry's body that was lying in the doorway of the room. A piece of packing tape was covering Mason's mouth. His hands were behind him, and Sato assumed they were taped also.

By now, Sato had stepped out of the alley and into the laundry. "Where the hell did you get the tape?"

"Oh, I noticed it when we were in here earlier. Had no idea it would still work, but it was worth a try. It worked."

"Keep your gun on him a second," Spencer said as he knelt and placed his hand on the neck of the man lying in the doorway. He looked up at Sato and said, "Our Heineken distributor has finished delivering his last beer. He's dead. It's the least we could do for Agent Wilson."

Spencer stood up and repeated Sato's earlier observation. "OK let's get the hell out of here."

Spencer ripped the tape off Mason's mouth. The painful yell was an indication that it was obviously not meant to be used on human skin. An oversight that Spencer seemed to be comfortable with.

Spencer turned to Sato and said, "Walking down the street with someone who has tape over their mouth might raise some questions. Now he just looks like a drunk who got in a fight."

Spencer grabbed Mason's arm and said, "I'm really not in a good mood right now, you son-of-a-bitch, so if you open your mouth while we are getting out of here, I will very happily empty the remaining rounds in this gun in your back. Do you understand me?" He jammed the gun into Mason's very sore rib.

Mason grimaced and said, "Yes."

"Good."

Sato led the way out of the laundry into the alley.

Spencer handed Sato his World War II Nambu. "Wipe it clean and put it in the bartender's hand.

Sato pulled a handkerchief from his back pocket, unfolded it and took the pistol. He wiped Spencer's prints from the gun. He then released the clip, wiped it clean and removed the remaining bullets and put them in his pocket. He replaced the clip and placed the gun in the hand of the unconscious man who had just tried to kill him.

Spencer had removed his Smith & Wesson from his shoulder holster and was holding it in Mason's back.

Sato made sure the bartender's prints covered the gun. He finally placed the man's trigger finger on the trigger and pushed it to fire the empty weapon. With the gun still positioned in Yuto's hand, Sato stood up.

He then aimed his Nambu at Yuto and pulled the trigger. After the blast the three men could see that a portion of the bartenders skull was missing.

Mason yelled, 'What the fuck!"

"Now is not the time for a witness," Sato said.

It was then that they saw a small group of people gathering at the entrance to the alley pointing and yelling.

"Jesus Christ!" Spencer cried out. "Go!"

Spencer grabbed Mason's arm, and the three men walked quickly toward the street.

The sound of police sirens in the distance didn't help to calm the situation. Just as they got to the end of the alley, a car pulled up and stopped directly in front of them, scattering the crowd.

The front passenger side window was open. The driver, who was wearing a black suit and a black brimmed fedora, leaned over and yelled out the window, "I suggest you get in the car now."

Spencer glanced at the growing crowd; many were pointing at them and yelling. The sound of police sirens was getting closer. It was not the position they wanted to be in.

Spencer pulled open the back door; pushed Mason in and got in behind him. Mason moaned in pain as he was pushed across the seat. Sato was already in the front passenger seat. The car began moving just as Spencer was pulling the door closed. The noise of the crowd quickly disappeared while the police car siren began to fade in the distance. No one spoke until the car had turned a corner and had gone several blocks.

Sato turned and looked back at Spencer.

"Agent Spencer, allow me to introduce Cheng Yu-hsuan.

The driver of the car looked in the mirror at Spencer and spoke. "I have been following you since you landed in Japan, Agent Spencer. Madam Li has a personal interest in your time in Japan."

"Well, without your help, Mr. Cheng, we would most likely have been in the hands of the police right now. Thank you."

Mr. Cheng nodded.

"Gentlemen, I'm guessing you have a planned destination for this ride." Spencer inquired.

Cheng glanced back again and said, "We are going to an empty warehouse near the docks. It is safe."

CHAPTER 17

January 10, 1968

As Cheng continued driving, the flashing neon lights, and frenetic crowds of Sasebo's bar area transitioned to a dimly lit two lane road paralleling the harbor. Large warehouses were sporadically positioned between the harbor and the road. A cargo ship could be seen being unloaded at one of the active quays. Huge cranes were delicately lifting shipping containers from the bowels of the giant vessel and setting them on the dock. The constant, almost choreographed movements of the longshoremen were spotlighted in the high intensity arc lamps.

The warehouses were becoming fewer and farther between. Cheng eventually pulled the car into the driveway of one of the distant buildings. The headlights were turned off and he drove slowly around the side of the building. The reflection of the bright moon off the choppy waters of the bay cast an eerie presence as the moving shadows enveloped the large steel warehouse. Pulling behind the building he came to a stop in front of a large roller shutter door. The door immediately began to open. He waited until it was raised to just above the height of the car and then slowly pulled into the building. Once inside, he stopped the car and shut off the engine.

“Gentlemen, we have arrived.” Cheng announced. “Please remain in the car until the garage door is closed and the lights are turned on. There are two men already in this building. They are with me.”

The whining of an electric motor began and the clanking and squeaking of the large door sections riding suspended roller tracks eventually ended with a thud as the door reached the concrete floor. The lights in the warehouse were turned on. Two men, dressed in dark suits were standing near the wall to the left of the roller shutter door. A black car was parked directly behind them.

“We are safe here, for now.” Cheng said as he opened his door and stepped out. The other men followed.

The cavernous warehouse they found themselves in was cluttered with abandoned steel shipping containers, piles of wooden pallets, large, flattened cardboard boxes, and rows of empty shelving.

The air was cool and damp and heavy. It smelled of wet concrete, oil, cardboard and rust.

Cheng walked around the car to Spencer and asked quietly, “May I have a word with you alone agent Spencer?” Spencer followed him away from the other men so that they would not be overheard.

“I understand that because of this situation you find yourself in, Agent Spencer, Madam Li has requested that following your ‘discussion’ with him, we might come to an arrangement where your Navy Captain would be turned over to us.”

Spencer glanced back at Mason momentarily and then returned his attention to Cheng.

"You are aware that one of Madam Li's top agents was brutally tortured and murdered because of information that an American passed to North Korea. She is willing to pay handsomely for the opportunity to take him into custody."

Spender asked, "But do we know yet if he is the man she is looking for?"

"Agent Spencer, the man who witnessed the torture and murder of our agent is Mr. Sato. He knew immediately when Mason walked into the bar that he was the man."

Spencer was surprised to hear that the witness was Sato. He wondered why he hadn't mentioned it before but was not going to question his reasoning. It didn't matter at this point.

Now knowing for certain that Mason was the man Madam Li had been searching for certainly solved the dilemma of how he could be stopped. Spencer knew that he was in no position to bring Mason to justice, but, at the same time, he could not let him go free. Madam Li's offer would solve both of those concerns.

Spencer looked at Mr. Cheng and said, "If my questioning goes as I expect it will, we have an arrangement. And there is certainly no need for payment."

"Excellent, Agent Spencer. Thank you."

Cheng pointed to his left toward an enclosed, doored cubical. "This office should provide you the privacy you require. To be safe, I would suggest you take as little time as needed."

"I understand."

Spencer walked back to Mason and firmly took hold of his left arm. "This way, Mason," he said as he pulled him toward the office. Mason grimaced in pain.

The small room was windowless. Spencer turned on the light as they entered. An old, dusty, wooden desk with a dilapidated swivel chair sat across from the door. A table with two wooden chairs, one on either side, sat in the middle of the room. A single glass light fixture with only one of the three bulbs still working hung from the ceiling above the table by a single chain. An old calendar and two dated Japanese posters were hanging on the otherwise empty walls. The air was stuffy and thick with dust.

Spencer shut the door behind them.

"Sit down Mason." He said, in a voice that implied he wasn't going to say it twice. Mason sat down. Spencer sat across from him. He pulled his Smith & Wesson from his holster and placed it on the table.

As he looked at Mason, the magnitude of the situation struck him again. He had just kidnapped a highly decorated United States Naval officer and carted him to an abandoned building in the shipping warehouse district of Sasebo, Japan. The fact that he and Sheila were the only two people in the Bureau who were aware that the man sitting across from him had been selling top secret United States military information to foreign countries for over a decade made the situation appear untenable. He realized, more than ever, that he was balancing on a very high tightrope without a net. He also realized that there was no turning back at this point.

Spencer understood that this man was, in fact, a treacherous and skilled saboteur. As a highly decorated Naval officer, he had continued to receive accolades and promotions for years from the very people who were entrusting him with top secret military secrets, while he, in turn, continued to sell those very secrets to our enemies

And Spencer was cognizant of the fact that Mason would not be held accountable for any of the crimes he had committed, as no military or civilian court in the country would find him guilty. He had taken great care to cover his tracks, making it impossible for any allegations against him to be substantiated.

Having the confirmation of an agreement with Mr. Chen brought a slight sense of relief, but he was fully aware that he and Sheila were still very vulnerable to being exposed if circumstances were to go awry.

Mason was sitting in the chair with his hands pushed against both legs attempting to ease the pain from the cracked rib.

"You understand why you are here, don't you?" Spencer began.

"You have assaulted and kidnapped a United States military officer. Do you understand what kind of trouble you are in agent? They did call you agent, didn't they? Let me guess, you are with the FBI. Does that sound right?"

"Tell me about the Pueblo, Mason." Spencer continued, undeterred.

"What's the Pueblo? Never heard of it."

"Two things, Captain Mason. First, I know you've been working as a spy for multiple countries for over a decade; and second - and this should be of much more importance to you right now - is that it's been a very long day; I'm tired, and I'm pissed, and I don't plan on making a fucking career out of playing word games with you. Do you have any idea what the projectile from this magnum will do to your kneecap?"

Mason tensed.

"OK, I know the Pueblo. A lot of people know about the Pueblo. It's sailing out of Sasebo this week. I understand it's headed to North Korea, but you already know that don't you? And I'm betting you would really like to stop it from sailing, wouldn't you?"

Spencer didn't respond.

"You have no idea who or what you're dealing with here do

you, agent? Do you think I can just pick up the phone and call someone to stop the Pueblo from sailing? There's no way in hell that's going to happen."

For someone who had been kidnapped, had his rib cracked and is setting across the table from a guy with a Smith and Wesson at the ready, his arrogance was astounding.

Spencer remained quiet.

"And you do realize that anything I say will be of no value to you, don't you? It's just you and me in this room. You will have no proof of anything, other than my word, and that will be useless for you."

"Tell me something about the Pueblo I don't know." Spencer continued, unshaken.

"OK, Agent, let's cut to the chase. You caught me. I am a spy, and I have been working for other countries for years, making millions of dollars doing it. And yes, I have been coordinating the planning of moving this ship to North Korea. But again, the only thing you are going to get out of this is my word and it will get you nowhere. You see Agent, I don't make mistakes. I always cover my tracks."

At this point, it seemed that Mason felt he was taking control of the interrogation.

"But let's look at the big picture here, Agent. Kidnapping a naval officer should get you a minimum of twenty years in prison – probably a lot more. And just who were you planning to go to with your wild story about me being a spy? I have worked for many of the highest-ranking officers in the Navy, and I would bet that not one of them would want to come forward and admit that an embedded spy worked for years directly under their command. Guessing it's not something any one of them would want to take ownership of."

"Mason, you do realize that there's nothing to stop me from killing you right now?"

"If you were going to kill me, you would have done it in the alley. I read people well, Agent. And I read you as a tough, by-the-book FBI agent - a follow the rules, underpaid government servant. There's no way you would kill me. And, besides, you still want information from me."

It was true, Spencer did still want information, but he had enough now, and they needed to get out of the warehouse.

"Are you starting to get the feeling that all of this evening was really a big mistake, Agent Spencer?"

"I don't." Spencer replied.

"Really, just who did you think you could go to with anything I tell you? Not a person will believe you. You have absolutely no proof of anything. I told you I don't make mistakes. I've been getting paid handsomely for selling top secret United States government information for years – became very, very rich doing it – and the only thing that could possibly come out of all of this is you getting old behind bars. I know you aren't going to kill me, and as it stands you really can't turn me in. You would be arrested immediately."

He continued with his still smug, cocky attitude. He sat back in his chair and smiled.

"Bet that really pisses you off, doesn't it? I have confessed to being a spy and there's not a goddamned thing you or anyone else can do about it because you have no proof."

He looked at Spencer and laughed. It was a laugh filled with condescension.

"But Agent, I have to say, kudos for finding me – the only other man who tracked me down is now twenty-five thousand feet deep in the Mariana Trench, assuming the sharks didn't get him. But you are still alive, at least for now. I can only applaud your efforts."

Spencer shifted in his seat and Mason read it as a sign of concern on his part.

"Look, Agent Spencer, you and I both know you can't go any further with this. Why don't we just get up and walk out of here. You can tell your buddies out there that this was all a big mistake, and you need to get me back to my base."

By now he was leaning on the table seemingly explaining to Spencer how things were going to go from there.

"If we do that Agent, I'll make you a very rich man. You get me back to my base and one hundred thousand dollars will be yours. Do you realize how that much money could change your life.

Spencer remained quiet.

"Look, you're obviously a smart guy," Mason continued, "and under the circumstances it's a win/win for both of us. I go back to the base, and you can start living the good life. We can just go our separate ways, forget tonight ever happened and no one will be the wiser."

"Sorry Mason, I can't accept your money."

"Why the hell not," Mason asked while looking somewhat shocked. "You're turning down one hundred thousand dollars? OK, let's up it to two hundred thousand. It's two hundred thousand dollars and it will all be yours. All you need to do is say yes, and you'll have enough money to retire and begin enjoying the good life."

Spencer slowly clasped his hands, rested them on the table and leaned forward.

"It's not that I'm turning it down Mason, it's just that you don't have the money to give me."

"I've got the money. Two hundred thousand dollars is a drop in the bucket for me. If I say you'll get the money, you'll get the money."

Spencer leaned back in his chair again; looked Mason directly in the eyes and asked, "Are we talking about the sixteen million dollars you have in the bank account in Hong Kong?"

Mason's cocky, assured expression collapsed immediately to a blank stare. His face turned ashen.

Spencer continued. "Well, I hope that wasn't your retirement nest egg Captain Mason, because yesterday all of that money was moved out of your account."

Mason replied in a frantic tone. "What do you mean it was moved out of the account? There's no way in hell you can do that!"

Spencer continued calmly. "I know this must come as quite a shock what with all the effort you put in to keeping it hidden – yes, covering your tracks. It's a shame, isn't it? You've been selling top secret United States military information to other countries for over ten years and all the money you made for it is gone."

"That's bullshit! There's no way you can move that money!"

Actually, Mason, I can move the money, and I did. Oh, it's a little tricky, and maybe not all above board, but it is doable.

"You're lying Spencer!! There's no fucking way that can happen!!"

"Unfortunately for you, it did happen. I did transfer the sixteen and a half million dollars out of your account, and it is now empty. It's kind of a perfect plan don't you think, because other than you, and me, no one else knows the money even exists. The account will be closed, I have all your money, and how did you put it - no one will be the wiser. Guess it's not the win/win you were hoping for, but it sure is a hell of a big win for me, don't you think? You know, for a brilliant guy who doesn't make any mistakes, losing sixteen million dollars sounds like a doozy to me." Spencer concluded, smiling.

By this time, Mason looked like he had lost his mind. He lunged across the table for the Smith & Wesson. Spencer grabbed his arm with his left hand, and with his right he slammed Mason's head into the table. Mason's forward motion was stopped immediately.

"Just so you know Mason, even a low-paid government servant like me tries not to make mistakes either. The gun is empty."

Spencer released his arm and lifted his hand from Mason's head. Mason sat up slowly. His nose was bloodied; his cheek was badly bruised, and his right arm seemed to be cocked in a strange position. He fell back into his chair.

"You know Mason, you are correct on one thing, though. I am going to have to let you go, because other than your confession - that we both know you will deny - I really have absolutely no proof that will stand up in court."

The room became quiet. Mason had bumped the light above the table, and it continued to swing back and forth slowly casting foreboding shadows in the stale, dust filled cubicle. Spencer stood up. "Let's go, Mason. Time to get you out of here."

"Then you are going to release me?" Mason asked hesitantly.

"Yes, I am."

The two men walked out of the room.

Cheng and one of the other men who had been standing near the warehouse door walked toward Spencer and Mason.

Spencer spoke first. "Mr. Cheng, the questioning went as

expected. We have an arrangement."

"Thank you, Agent Spencer. Now the sooner we get out of here the better."

Cheng's man grabbed Mason's arm. Mason's eyes grew wide with fear.

Spencer then turned toward Mason and said, "You were right that even with your confession there is nothing I can do to stop you – you've outsmarted the Navy and the United States Government. I must give you that – you are a bright guy. You got us. But just because there is nothing I can do, Mason, it certainly doesn't preclude these gentlemen from going forward with an investigation of their own."

Mason tensed. "What the hell are you talking about? What investigation? I demand to be taken back to my base." His voice was panicked.

"These men are from Taiwan. I think you might know something about one of their agents being brutally tortured and murdered about a year ago. What you don't know is that one of their other agents had infiltrated the North Koreans and just happened to be there the night the torture and murder took place.

You probably don't recognize this gentleman standing to your right, but he was there with you when you tortured and killed that man. And, as it turns out, he has identified you. They now have proof you are the man they have been looking for. And you Captain Mason, as you have explained to me numerous times this evening, know how important it is to have proof. So, it turns out that even though there is nothing at all I can do to stop you, just knowing that you confessed everything to me is going to make it so much easier for me to hand you over to them. And if you are as smart as you think you are, and haven't made any additional mistakes, you'll be back at the Officer's club having a drink with your buddies before you know it."

"Wait, you can't hand me over to them. We've got a deal!" Mason screamed. "Jesus Christ! You bastard! I'm a highly decorated officer in the United States Navy. You won't get away with this."

"Well, when you get back to base, you can contact the authorities."

"In the meantime, we all must get out of here. This is where I bid you adieu Captain Mason"

Mr. Cheng's man roughly pulled the still screaming Mason to the black sedan parked near the large roller shutter door.

Spencer then turned to Mr. Sato and reached out his hand. Sato reached out his hand in return, and with one of his rare smiles said, "Thank you agent Spencer. It seems the bargirls were right all along."

Spencer smiled as they released their handshake. "It seems they were, Mr. Sato. Good luck my friend."

Spencer walked to the second car with Mr. Cheng. Before he closed the car door, he glanced over to the other car. The driver was behind the wheel and Mason was in the back seat with Sato. The third man turned off the lights in the warehouse and opened the garage door. The whining of the electric motor began again and the clanking and squeaking of the large door sections riding the suspended roller tracks continued until the door was fully open. The last man got into the front seat of the other car and then both cars drove out of the warehouse with their headlights off.

"Agent Spenser, where can I take you?"

"I must get to the airport in Nagasaki for a flight to Tokyo, but that's over an hour away. Can you get me to a bus station?"

"Best for me to drive you. Safer that way. No problem at all."

"Are you sure Mr. Cheng?"

"Consider it I owe you for Captain Mason." Mr. Cheng turned toward Spencer and smiled.

As they pulled onto the road, the bright moon was still reflecting off the waves in the harbor. A ship's horn could be heard declaring its position out beyond the bay and several quays were still active with longshoreman unloading large freighters. They sat quietly as Mr. Cheng drove to Nagasaki. It had been a very long day.

CHAPTER 18

Spencer was settled in a chair in the boarding area of the airport in Nagasaki waiting for his flight to Tokyo. He glanced at his watch; he had just over six hours until his flight out of Tokyo to Honolulu was scheduled for departure and he needed to be on that flight.

He had recently killed a man in an alley in bar town in Sasebo and had kidnapped a Navy Captain, interrogated him and then turned him over to a Taiwanese spy organization. The chances of connecting him with the murder and kidnapping were very slim, but still he was understandably anxious. There could not be any delay on the Nagasaki to Tokyo flight.

He sat quietly and waited.

The announcement finally came that his plane would begin boarding.

Spencer found his seat and settled in. Although he was more than an hour out of Sasebo, he was aware that at any time police could come walking down the aisle to remove him from the plane. His seat was next to the window, and he casually pulled the window shade down, picked up the inflight magazine and waited for the plane to take off.

He was finally in the air, and his normal breathing pattern returned. The flight to Tokyo was just under two hours. The physical and mental exhaustion of the past couple of days had caught up with him. He returned the magazine to the seat organizer in front of him and fell asleep almost immediately.

The plane arrived in Tokyo on time. He followed the signs to his departure gate to Honolulu, found an open seat in the passenger waiting area and sat down. He was a little less anxious now that he was in Tokyo.

The boarding area was filled with passengers scheduled for a flight to Australia that was leaving several hours before his. He noticed that the children were still active, while the parents just looked frazzled. He was happy to be missing that flight.

When the ticket counter opened for his flight, he was one of the first in line. The agent checked his passport and ticket and then turned to check with a lady who appeared to be his supervisor. They seemed to be studying his ticket with much interest. Several minutes passed. Spencer tried to look calm, but he could only assume his name had been tagged in Sasebo, and he would be stopped from leaving the country.

"Mr. Spencer?" the lady asked.

"Yes, I'm James Spencer," he replied.

"It appears that you have been upgraded to first class. Allow my associate to print out your new ticket and thank you for flying Japan Air Lines."

The agent smiled as he returned Spencer's passport with the new upgraded ticket. He took his passport and first-class ticket, stepped back to the boarding area and found a seat. He thought perhaps he would always use Sheila as his travel agent.

The plane began loading and Spencer settled into his upgraded first-class seat. He found himself waiting again, somewhat anxiously, for the plane to depart. The plane doors were finally closed, and the overhead speaker announced, first in Japanese and then English, that all seat backs should be in the upright position, and seatbelts should be fastened.

The plane jerked slightly as the pushback tractor backed the plane away from the terminal. The flight was exactly on time. After a disconnect from the tractor and a flurry of flashlight waving from the ground crew, the Japan Air Lines DC-8 filled with 189 passengers taxied to the runway.

And then it stopped.

The plane sat on the tarmac for thirty minutes. It was thirty minutes that Spencer could have lived without. He wondered again if the authorities had somehow caught up with him and ordered the plane to return to the terminal to have him removed? He sat quietly.

One is seldom given an official explanation as to why planes are delayed before takeoff, but the rumor spread quickly that debris had been spotted on the runway they were using. It was as good a guess as any. Spencer focused on that possibility.

The speakers finally came to life and the pilot first apologized for the delay and then reported that they had just been given clearance to take off. A few people applauded while a collective sigh of relief could be sensed from the rest of the passengers – Spencer included.

"Please make sure that your seatbelts are fastened, and your seat backs are in the upright position. And again, thank you for flying with Japan Air Lines."

The four engines roared loudly as the large jet made a very rapid ascend. It was a clear indication that the pilot had no intentions of arriving in Honolulu late. The plane reached cruising altitude within 15 minutes and the seat belt sign was turned off. The sky-blue uniformed stewardesses were already busy preparing for the evening meal as two of their team members pushed the liquor cart down the aisle and began handing out drinks. The in-flight meal that evening for first class passengers included Chicken Kiev or steak with Sauce Diane - served on fine table linen with Royal Doulton china. The champagne was Dom Pérignon and dessert was a choice of either Crème Brulee or chocolate torte. The flight had just become even a bit more comfortable.

As Spencer was waiting for dinner, he picked up the in-flight magazine and browsed through it. According to an article he chanced upon, the sky-blue uniforms of the stewardesses were new for Japan Air Lines. They had switched to the new style and color with the launch of Japan Air Lines first westward round-the-world service flight in March of 1967. The airlines felt that the new uniforms would help commemorate the occasion.

Spencer glanced from the article to the stewardesses. He felt that the airline had made an excellent choice.

Spencer finished his meal and asked the attendant who was removing his tray if he might have a Dewar's with no ice and a just a splash of water. She smiled and quickly returned with his drink.

He slowly sipped his scotch realizing he was finally safe. It was a good feeling. He finished his drink, turned off his reading light, leaned back in his lush, soft leather first-class seat, and fell asleep.

CHAPTER 19

The quiet, dimmed cabin of the DC-8 came to life as the overhead lights were switched on and the captain announced that the plane would be landing in Honolulu in 30 minutes.

Spencer glanced at his watch. It was 0045 hours.

He lifted the shade on the window next to him and looked out at the clusters of lights that dotted the otherwise pitch-black landscape.

Spencer had just returned from a trip which, aside from Sheila, he would never divulge to anyone. There would be no mandatory debriefing or post-trip summary. It was four days that would be lost forever.

Despite knowing the slim chances of success in both locating the naval spy and stopping the departure of the Pueblo, Spencer remained resolute in his decision to attempt it. From his point of view, the mission was not a failure as he effectively eradicated two saboteurs who had cleverly eluded the Navy's surveillance for over a decade. Additionally, it served as a form of justice for the killing of Agent Wilson.

But the Pueblo would sail, reaching a location near the North

Korean International Maritime Boundary. As Mason had openly shared in his interrogation in the warehouse, the location would allow for easy capture by the North Korean Navy.

Due to a lack of competent, focused leadership on the part of the United States Navy, the entire cache of highly classified United States cryptographic equipment and documentation on board would soon fall into the hands of the Soviet Union. The United States Navy had managed to facilitate one of the biggest security breaches in American history. Not their finest hour.

The hunt, though, was over for Spencer and Anderson. Their unauthorized investigation into the collaborative spy operations in Virginia and Japan had come to an end. They had reached that point where they knew it was time to step away.

"Enough with these games," he said to himself.

He and Sheila were planning to move on with their lives and not look back. They had decided that he would continue in his position with the FBI in Hawaii until his retirement from the Bureau. Sheila would remain in Washington for one more month to ensure that there was no indication either of them was in the bureau's sights. She would then leave the FBI and move to Hawaii with Spencer. After years of avoiding a serious relationship, even one month apart seemed too long for both of them now, but they understood it was necessary.

The plane touched down softly on the runway and taxied to the terminal. Even before it came to a complete stop at the gate, the passengers behind the demarcation curtain jumped to their feet to retrieve their luggage from the overhead bins and then waited bunched together in somewhat awkward positions in the aisle until the boarding bridge was securely in place and the plane door was opened.

The first-class section moved in a somewhat more orderly fashion as the passengers casually exited the huge jet before the herd was released. James followed the signs to customs. Anticipating a long delay, he was pleasantly surprised how quickly he was processed. So, with stamped passport and carry-on luggage in hand he headed to ground transportation.

His plan had always been to take a few extra days away from the office, following his return, to find an apartment for Sheila and him. Together they had decided that an apartment would give them the flexibility to become accustomed to the surrounding neighborhoods before they looked for a house.

Spencer arrived back at the hotel that evening, exhausted. He placed his suitcase on the stand near the door, undressed, turned out the lights and collapsed into bed. He slept until ten that morning.

The next afternoon found him sitting in a realtor's office flipping through pictures of apartments for rent. He settled on two to look at. The second one, he felt, was perfect for them. It was a single-story duplex with a covered patio in the back, and a privacy fence that enclosed the small back yard. It was in a quiet neighborhood not far from the office. He signed the paperwork and would be moving in as soon as his belongings arrived from the states. The new apartment was, understandably, a big part of the conversation on the next phone call with Sheila. For some reason the two of them being together just seemed so much more real now.

"Welcome back, Sir." Agent Coleman cheerfully said as he stepped into the office the following morning.

"Good morning, Agent Coleman. And thank you."

"I hope your time off gave you some time to explore our beautiful island. And, if you don't mind me asking; did you have any luck finding an apartment?"

"I don't mind, and yes, I did. It's only about twenty minutes from here, and it's in a nice neighborhood."

"Excellent." She responded, again smiling. "And things have been very quiet while you were gone."

"Well, that's always a good thing."

"Oh, before I forget, here are some messages and mail that came in for you," she said while handing him several notes and envelopes.

"Thanks, Agent Coleman, let's hope it remains quiet." He responded with a smile.

He closed his office door behind him and sat down. Laying the notes and mail on his desk he then pulled open the top right drawer and removed the black and white framed snapshot of the chartered fishing boat trip and studied it. The photo was of no use now, and Wilson's widow might find the picture comforting. Spencer realized that there was nothing he could possibly share with his widow about what really happened. The investigation had found the explosion to be an accident, and it was important that it be left at that.

He stood up with the picture, carried it to the spot on the wall it once occupied and hung it back.

He then stepped back to his desk, picked up his SPAM coffee mug and headed to the coffee table. He was glad to see the bag of Kona coffee next to the pot. Occasionally a stateside coffee would appear, and it just wasn't the same. He hated to say it, but Maxwell House just didn't compare to the flavor of the Hawaiian Kona.

A hot cup of Kona coffee; the day was looking up.

That evening, after everyone had left the office, Spencer removed Agent Wilson's file from under the desk file drawer and walked to the paper shredder in the main office. He carefully removed each page from the file and ran it through the shredder. He then finished by feeding the manila folder into the cutter blades. He bagged the destroyed evidence and tossed it down the trash receptacle next to the elevator on his way out.

As he rode down to the lobby, he reflected again on Agent Wilson's excellent work that had enabled him to stop Mason and Curry. He wished he had had the opportunity to have known the man.

Spencer became comfortable with his new position in Honolulu, and as the weeks passed, everything began to fall into place. It would have been easy to just go through the motions required to do the job, but he never lost track of the important responsibilities of the position, and he always conducted himself accordingly. But his respect for the Bureau had ended on that Tuesday in Washington.

It was exactly two weeks after his arrival in Hawaii when his furniture and car arrived from the states. He took a couple of extra days off to get settled into his – their – new apartment.

James and Sheila spoke on the phone at least three times a week, both counting the days until they could be together again. One of the things they discussed was that Sheila shouldn't tell anyone she was moving to Hawaii, and she shouldn't get a job when she got there until things were completely quiet. This concerned James, more than Sheila, but she understood her career would have to be put on hold for a while. They were both extremely excited about her move over but were also acutely aware that they were not yet out of the woods from possible detection. They could still be facing the fate of Allston Sidwell if they were discovered, even now. As such, their telephone conversations continued to be conducted between a random pay phone in Hawaii and a deli just outside of Washington DC. They talked about everything. They joked years later about how many quarters they must have gone through over those four weeks.

According to Sheila, the Washington Field Office had been quiet and the navy spy in Norfolk who was selling secret cryptographic codes to the Soviets in Washington DC was a non-story. The US Government and the FBI had succeeded in whitewashing any traces of the rumors. John Walker continued to sell secret information to the USSR, but it was not to be mentioned again - until years later.

The highly decorated naval captain, stationed in Japan, whose stellar career was founded on a decade of espionage against our country, had received numerous

professional and religious gatherings of recognition and remembrance, as Spencer had expected. His failure to return from Sasebo, was ultimately written off as a local crime incident.

As the weeks passed, the clandestine phone calls between James and Sheila continued until she finally turned in her notice at the Bureau. Her explanation for leaving was that her mother had taken ill and needed constant attention. Her mother was, in fact, in excellent health, but the story worked, and her resignation raised no suspicions.

She and her mother had always been very close and talked on the phone almost weekly, and Sheila had never missed a chance to fly home for special holidays. James and Sheila felt that a stop at her mother's house for a visit for a few days was a wonderful idea, and it would give them both time to catch up before she continued her flight to Hawaii. Being as cautious as they both were, they realized that a direct flight to Hawaii also might have raised some flags at the Bureau, so a visit at home first was an excellent idea for several reasons.

The Honolulu airport that Saturday morning was crowded with tourists coming and going. James waited anxiously at the arrival gate. The announcement that had come over the loudspeakers several minutes earlier said that her plane had landed.

James watched as the passengers from her plane filed into the terminal. When she appeared, James moved forward to greet her. Sheila caught sight of him in the crowd and yelled. He ran toward her. When he reached her, he could see tears were welling up in her eyes. They embraced and kissed.

"James, I can't believe we are finally together." By now tears were running down her face.

As their extended embrace ended, James teasingly asked, "Are you ready to find that little Esso station, and just leave the world behind?"

"Do we get to park under a palm tree and spy on people before we go?" she asked, laughing.

"Well, that goes without saying." He replied with a grin.

"Oh my god, Sheila, you have no idea how happy I am to see you. Are you really here for good?"

"Well, for as long as you'll have me," she said smiling. "Let's get my suitcases and head to this lovely apartment you have told me so much about."

Sheila had left Washington with just two suitcases. Moving her furniture and car to Hawaii didn't make sense for the two of them. She donated her furniture to AMVET, and piles of clothes went to the Salvation Army. The super at her apartment bought her car. She was delighted at the prospect of rebuilding her wardrobe in Hawaii. It just seemed fitting seeing that she was beginning a brand-new chapter in her life with James.

They each carried a suitcase as they walked to the car. As they exited from the baggage claim area a lovely young lady dressed in a colorful blouse and a skirt made of ti leaves greeted them. "Aloha, welcome to Hawaii."

She placed a lei of carnation and jasmine blossoms around Sheila's neck.

"Thank you. How sweet." Sheila responded smiling brightly. She reached over and grabbed James's hand, and they continued walking.

James placed the suitcases in the trunk and then opened the passenger door for Sheila. "Your coach awaits my lady."

They talked continuously on the way to the apartment. It was if they were both trying to get as much in as they could before the pay phone ran out of coins. The weather was perfect, the traffic was light, and they couldn't have been happier.

Over the next few weeks, things settled down and they easily became accustomed to living together in paradise. They didn't talk about the recent past - the spies in Virginia and Hawaii, the Pueblo, James's trips to The Republic of China and Japan. They had moved on, and it just wasn't something that they wanted to occupy their time with. Every day seemed even more wonderful than the last. They couldn't have been happier.

Then, on a Friday afternoon, an envelope arrived that reopened a window to the past and was to change their lives forever.

Sheila had brought the mail in that day and sat it on the kitchen counter, which she often did. James picked up the mail when he got home from work that evening and sorted through it while Sheila was finishing dinner.

"That smells amazing, Honey."

"Why thank you kind sir." She responded.

"Oh, here's one for you." he said, as he handed her a forwarded envelope from the states.

"Wow, how did they actually get this to us in Hawaii?" she asked as she read the postal cover envelope. She opened the envelope to find a letter inside addressed to her old apartment. The post mark on the letter was from Hong Kong.

"James!"

"What is it?"

"This is a letter from Hong Kong."

"Hong Kong! From whom?" he asked.

"It doesn't have a return address," she said as she opened it.

The short, typed letter was dated almost exactly one month earlier. There was no opening salutation.

Sheila read the letter slowly.

"The final payment was posted to the account. It has been moved to the holding account. Original account closed. There is no record. Your friend."

They stood quietly for a few moments before Sheila said, "Thomas Chen. It's from Thomas."

Both were at a loss for words because they had, honestly forgotten about the account in Hong Kong. Their lives had been filled with enjoying everything about Hawaii and planning their future together. The bank account was nothing more than a line item in a case that had been closed in their minds.

"Oh my god," Sheila finally continued. "I forgot all about that account. Well, that's certainly good news. The old account has been closed and that chapter of the story has been erased."

"I can't believe I forgot about it too," James added. "You know, Thomas couldn't have been a better contact."

"And friend," Sheila added.

James continued going through the mail, tossing most of it into the waste basket.

"Now for some bad news, we got our electric and water bill. I hate bills." James set the unopened bills back on the counter with a small groan.

They had a leisurely dinner at the kitchen table that evening and talked about the day. James had had a rather uneventful end of the week, but Sheila had some exciting news about a new housing development of three-bedroom homes that she heard was being built only about ten miles from their apartment. She thought maybe they could drive by the next morning just to take a peek.

"I'm in!" James responded, with a smile. "Can we afford them do you think?"

"Well, if what I heard they would be going for is correct, we can. Might have to squeeze our budget a bit, but yep."

"Perfect!"

"Tomorrow will be a house hunting adventure." Sheila said cheerfully.

"A Saturday adventure. I love it." James responded with a grin.

"Are you ready for a glass of wine, Mr. Spencer?"

"I am and I will pour us a glass right now. Red or White?" He replied.

"Let me clean up the kitchen a bit, and I'll meet you on the patio. Oh, and red for me please."

It was a quiet evening, which was somewhat unusual for their neighborhood on a Friday. There always seemed to be a gathering somewhere on the block that usually involved loud music and adult beverages. But this night was quiet.

"I love Hawaii," James. "And I love our apartment – well, a three-bedroom house would be lovely too. We'll keep our fingers crossed."

"I have a feeling that tomorrow is going to be our lucky day. This new allotment you found could be perfect."

They looked at each other and smiled.

"A toast to a lucky day tomorrow."

"A toast to a lucky day tomorrow." He responded as they clicked their glasses.

They finished their wine as they sat chatting for almost an hour enjoying the warm evening breeze in their new paradise.

Sheila glanced at James and said, "Wonder what's on TV tonight? Maybe a good movie."

"I don't know, but I could go for a good movie too. And how about some popcorn and another glass of wine?"

"I'll check what's on. Do you need help with the popcorn or wine?"

"Nope, I got it."

Sheila yelled in from the living room. "We have a choice, The Glass Menagerie, or Casablanca. They both start at nine. Your choice."

"Casablanca, without a doubt!" James yelled back.

"You're just saying that because you know I love that movie."

"No, really, this is a Bogart night for sure."

They settled comfortably into their couch and shared the popcorn. They had both seen the movie so many times that they found themselves speaking the lines along with the cast. It became kind of a contest on who remembered the most lines. Sheila won. The movie ended, and they carried their empty wine glasses and popcorn bowl back to the kitchen and sat them on the counter. James pulled Sheila to him and kissed her warmly.

"Here's looking at you, kid." He said with a grin.

They turned off the lights as they walked to the bedroom. It had been another wonderful day in paradise.

"James, are you awake?" Sheila asked quietly.

"Huh. What. Oh yea, I'm awake. What time is it?"

"It's just after two," Sheila answered as she reached to turn on the lamp on the bedstand next to her side of the bed."

"What's the matter, Honey?" He asked, while trying to focus his eyes to the light.

"James, what's going to happen to the money when we die?"

"What money?" he asked somewhat incredulously.

"James, there is sixteen and a half million dollars setting in an account in Hong Kong. Well, maybe a lot more now. When we die, the money will still be in the account, right?"

"Yes, the money will still be in the account. What are you getting at?"

"And five hundred years from now it will still be there."

"I would imagine so, yes."

"Do you remember when we were in Washington, having pizza and scotch in the restaurant after you were stopped from finding the Navy spy and you found out you were being forced to move to Hawaii?"

"Yes."

"And we learned that the Bureau was behind Sidwell's murder and spy coverup and everything else?"

"Yes."

"And the next morning when we got up you said, they aren't going to beat us on this Sheila. No matter what happens, when all is said and done, we are going to be the ones who come out on top."

"Yes, I do. He replied with a sense of hesitation.

"Well, I just had a dream… I think we should keep the money."

The room became quiet. The shears over the open window were whispering softly in the light breeze. There was no other sound.

After what seemed like several minutes of silence, Sheila continued. "James, I have thought it through. There is absolutely no way anyone can find out about it. This just isn't me guessing; you do know I have a bit of experience in international finance." She smiled with a somewhat hesitant grin.

"Wait, you had a dream, and now you want to keep the money?"

"Yes. And you know me James, I would never do anything crazy."

"You don't think that taking sixteen million dollars is crazy?"

"No James, listen, basically, we find ourselves with millions of dollars in a bank account – our bank account – that can never be traced. Either we use the money, or it will still be sitting there in five hundred years. Don't you see, this is our path to come out on top. The only thing I don't like about it is that we would be the only ones who will know we beat them."

Sheila then became quiet, wondering how James was going to respond to her what seemed now like a proclamation. She probably shouldn't have brought it up. She could hardly breath.

Again, only the whispering of the shears.

The room remained quiet until James finely asked, "Would you like a cup of coffee? This sounds a little more serious than just pillow talk." And after another small hesitation, he smiled and said, "And, you know, Honey, perhaps a three-bedroom house might be a bit small after all."

Sheila started breathing again.

They sat at the kitchen table, drinking coffee and talking until four thirty that morning. They discussed every step of the process of safely moving the money so that it would be easily available to them and never traced. They both agreed that the money could never be returned or brought to the attention of the Navy or the United States Government.

What they were talking about doing certainly wasn't something that they would ever have considered if the situation was normal. But the situation was different, very different. They ultimately decided that leaving the untraceable funds in the account forever would be a huge mistake.

So very early on that Saturday morning James Spencer and Sheila Anderson decided to do something crazy. Unfortunately, no one was ever to know that they were the ones who came out on top.

CHAPTER 20

One month later.

The doorbell rang in a small, framed house just outside of Washington DC.

"Jim, there is someone at the door, do you want to get it?"

Jim looked at Macy, his face expressing both sadness and apprehension.

"Honey, do you think it's the bank?"

"I don't know. Let's just pray it isn't."

Jim walked to the door and slowly opened it, dreading what they might be faced with.

"Good afternoon," said the man standing on the porch. "Are you James Johnson?"

"Yes, I am," Jim answered with hesitation.

"I have three registered letters that need to be signed for."

James took the pen and the pad and signed the three mail receipts.

The delivery man thanked Jim, handed him the three envelopes and left.

Jim looked at the letters; one was from the hospital, and two were from the bank.
Why, he wondered, why did they all have to come together. His eyes started to tear up as he turned to Macy who was standing just inside in the doorway behind him. She grabbed his arm to help steady them both. She also had tears in her eyes as she said, "The good Lord works in mysterious ways, Jim. He will be there to help us through this."

Jim walked into the living room; Macy followed with her hand on his back. His walk and demeanor were of a much older man now. Macy tried to put on a brave face as she sat on the couch and patted the cushion next to her. "Come here, Jim. Let's do this together."

Jim sat down slowly.

He sat two of the letters on the coffee table and held the larger one in his hand, the bold return address seemed to jump out in an almost threatening way. First Savings and Loan.

Jim slowly opened the large manilla envelope and removed two documents. He began reading the cover letter.

He stopped reading and handed it to Macy.

Dear Mr. and Mrs. Johnson. As valued customers of ours for over 40 years we are delighted to share that your home loan had been repaid in full and your property deed is enclosed. There was more to the letter, but they didn't finish it.

"Jim, I don't understand. We were behind in our payments, and they were threatening to foreclose on the loan this month. I don't understand."

"I don't understand either, Macy. Can this be a mistake? Let me read it again."

They both read the letter together. Almost afraid to look at the enclosed document, Jim slowly pulled it from behind the cover letter. It was a signed and certified deed for their house in their names.

"Jim, this can't be right. They have made a mistake. We can't keep this."

Jim agreed.

"Let's open the other letters," he said, "and then we'll call the bank to let them know about this mistake."

He picked up the letter from the hospital, knowing that they were in arrears by over four thousand dollars. He read the first few lines of the cover letter and then moved to the enclosed invoice. He slowly handed it to Macy. The letter read: Dear Mr. and Mrs. Johnson. Enclosed is the final copy of your outstanding balance. The itemized invoice showed that the bill had been paid in full.

"Jim, something is wrong. This can't be true."

They looked at each other, not really knowing what to say. Macy then glanced down at the third letter.

"Jim, I'm afraid to open that one."

Jim picked up the envelope and slowly opened it. Again, it was from their Savings and Loan, but the return address didn't seem quite as ominous this time.

The letter informed them that a deposit to their account had been wired to the bank and their savings account had been credited with fifty thousand dollars.

By now, they both realized that none of this was a mistake. Someone had done this for them. They reached for each other and hugged as they both cried.

"Macy, the Lord does work in mysterious ways. Who would have done this for us?"

"I have no idea." She responded. Her tears had stopped, and she was smiling.

"This is God's doing, Jim. Perhaps someday we will find out, but that will be at his time."

While half a world away a phone rings in an office at a bank in Hong Kong. It is answered by a Mr. Thomas Chen

"Mr. Chen, my name is Liu Xiaochang. I am the President of Rolls Royce Motor Cars of Hong Kong, and I am calling to inform you that your luxury automobile is now available. I would like to invite you to join me for an exclusive appointment so that I might share with you, personally, the amazing features of this beautiful automobile.

"I'm sorry, perhaps you have the wrong number, I haven't ordered an automobile."

"I suspected that this might come as a surprise as your benefactor has requested complete anonymity, but we can assure you that we have received appropriate, certified documentation, in your name, for a brand-new Rolls Royce Phantom VI automobile that is to be delivered to you. The automobile has been paid for in full, and a lifetime warranty has been included.

There was silence on the line.

"Mr. Chen," the gentleman on the phone continued, "I must tell you that this is the finest automobile that we have ever procured through our establishment. And most interestingly, it is the exact model purchased by Queen Elizabeth."

Thomas loved surprises – especially expensive surprises. He wasn't about to miss the thrill of picking up a new Rolls Royce Phantom VI at Hong Kong's finest automobile emporium.

"I must tell you that I am totally shocked," Thomas finely responded, "But, yes of course I will be there within the hour. Thank you."

Thomas hung up the phone and slowly scrolled through the rolodex sitting on his large mahogany desk. He found the card for Sheila Anderson, removed it from the file, and placed it in his pocket.

He then sat back in his chair, smiled, and said quietly, "Thank you, my dear friend."

CHAPTER 21

Sheila and James were sitting on cushioned chairs under the vine covered pergola just off the cucina of their villa. The olive trees that lined the structure on two sides were in full bloom and the beautiful small white blossoms were sparkling in the morning sun. The light breeze that was softly rolling down from the vast hills of grape vines was pleasantly warm. This was their favorite spot for morning coffee.

Sheila, who was holding a newspaper stopped reading and sat the paper on her lap when their housemaid arrived with a fresh carafe of hot coffee and a selection of delicious looking pastries.

"Thanks, Maria." Sheila said with a wide smile.

"You are welcome," the cheerful, middle-aged lady replied. "Can I bring you anything else?"

"No, but you must take one of the pastries, Maria. They look delicious!"

She smiled sweetly and said thank you as she reached for one of the treats.

"Maria, if I were you," James interjected, smiling. "I'd go for the biggest one, or Sheila's going to grab it."

Maria was smiling as she walked off with a pastry. It appeared to be a large one.

James poured the coffee while Sheila picked up the newspaper and continued reading.

"What!" Sheila exclaimed. "James, have you read the paper yet?"

"I haven't. Why, what are you reading?"

"Here," she said, as she handed him a two-day old copy of the Corriere della Sera, turned to page three.
"Look below the fold."

James took the paper. It was dated May 21, 1985. It read, in Italian: Former U.S. Navy communications specialist arrested by the FBI for spying. It went on to say that John Anthony Walker had been selling classified documents to the Soviet Union for over 18 years. Authorities discovered that he began working with the Soviets while based at Naval Station Norfolk in Virginia in 1967. The United States Navy reported that there had been no account of his activities with the Soviets while stationed at Norfolk or any of his other assigned bases. They went on to say that the Navy would be following up with an extensive investigation of their own.

James looked at Sheila. "Eighteen years to finally catch him. My God. It certainly gives you a secure feeling doesn't it."

Sheila responded, "Eighteen years! I know you just want to scream too don't you, but we really can't let this bother us. It was from a different world a long, long time ago. And, I hate to say it, but if you had caught him then - which you would have – we certainly wouldn't have been living all these years in this beautiful villa in Italy. And we wouldn't have had our dear Maria bringing us these delicious pastries every morning."

"You're right, of course, Honey. We know that we did what we could. It's just a shame that no one will ever know what really happened."

After a moment of silence he added, "What do you think about writing a book telling the whole story?"

"Who, me?" Sheila responded.

"Well, I was thinking about me, but I will be needing a top-notch editor." He replied, smiling.

"I would be delighted to be your top-notch editor, but might I suggest one thing?"

"Wait, already rewriting my prose?" He laughed.

"No, sweetheart. My only suggestion is that we don't publish it for another thirty or forty years."

James thought for a moment and then replied, "They probably don't have pastries like this in prison do they. OK, let's shoot for thirty or forty years.

They each picked up their cup of coffee and James said, "A toast to thirty or forty years."

"A toast to thirty or forty years." They both repeated.

Smiling, they clicked their coffee cups and then quietly went on with their perfect lives. They were, as you say, on top.

The End

Printed in Dunstable, United Kingdom

79542604R00127